OUTSHONE

HER ROYAL HAREM: EMBER
BOOK THREE

CATHERINE BANKS

TURBO KITTEN INDUSTRIES

Outshone by Catherine Banks

Cover design by Bewitching Book Covers.
Formatted by Turbo Kitten Industries™
Published by Turbo Kitten Industries™

Turbo Kitten Industries™

P.O. Box 5012, Galt, CA 95632

HER ROYAL HAREM

EMBER

3

OUTSHONE

USA TODAY BESTSELLING AUTHOR

CATHERINE BANKS

CHAPTER ONE

Having the man you are dating livid with you is never a nice experience. It's ten times worse when there are four of them and one of them is the alpha and king of your pack.

"Thank you. Thank you so much," the petite, weasel shifter hybrid woman we had rescued repeated over and over again as she bowed before me.

"I'm just glad you're safe," I told her as my heart hammered in my chest and my lungs burned. I'd just woken to find myself in Leona's yard, successfully rescued by Kieran and carried to safety.

"Ember!" Leona shouted as she ran out of the house. She dropped to her knees in front of me and hugged me tightly. "Are you okay? They all fell through and we didn't see you and they all started freaking out and we were so worried!"

I patted her back. "I'm ... good. Just ... weak."

"She passed out as soon as I grabbed her," Kieran answered. "Remained unconscious until we landed."

"Thank you for getting me here safely."

He smiled. "You're welcome, Em."

"Caleb, what's wrong with you?" Leona snapped. "Your girlfriend saved your lives and you're treating her like she is your enemy right now."

"You teleported everyone, but you," Caleb said, snarling.

Caleb, Riddick, Branson, and Triston stood tensely, fists clenched, glaring at me.

"I couldn't make another portal and I wasn't going to abandon her." I didn't know her name, but thankfully everyone knew who I was talking about.

"What if Kieran hadn't been there?" Riddick hissed.

"I was escaping," I told them and stood. My legs wobbled and I almost fell, but righted myself before Leona could reach out to steady me. "I made it almost to the street." I understood that they were upset that I had almost sacrificed myself, but we were all safe.

They continued to glare at me, silent.

"You know what, fine, be mad at me. All that matters is that you are all safe and no one got fucking decapitated!" Turning, I stomped around the house and out to the front yard, waiting for Ezio or Martin, whoever was going to come pick us up.

Jolie and Nico popped into existence near me. Had I had any energy, I might have startled.

"Ember!" Jolie gasped and ran to me, sliding on her knees in the grass in her hurry. "Are you okay? What happened?"

As she held me, genuine concern in her voice, I broke. Tears spilled down my face and I sobbed.

"Where are the others?" Nico asked softly.

"In the back," I hiccup sobbed. "Alive and still assholes."

Nico left and Jolie stroked my hair. "What happened?"

"We were losing, Jolie. They were about to cut Caleb's head off. Everyone was about to die. I-I teleported them, but couldn't make one for myself. I started escaping and Kieran found me. Kieran saved me and brought me here. They're so mad. I admitted I love them and all they're doing right now is glaring at me. They haven't even touched me or anything. They are just mad."

"Oh, honey, they're just dealing with the emotions of thinking they might have lost you. Give them a bit to calm down. The adrenaline is pouring through them. It'll wear off."

My tears spent, I wiped my face and stood. "Right, sorry. The adrenaline and magic drain got to me for a moment, too."

Two SUVs pulled up and Jolie tugged me towards the first one with Martin driving. "Come on, let's get you home."

Jolie and I climbed into the SUV.

"Ember!" Triston called.

"Can we go?" I asked Martin, huddling in on myself, feeling cold and hollow.

He glanced at Jolie, who nodded.

"Yes, ma'am," he said and started driving.

"We're going to take you to the house where Kara is waiting," Jolie informed me as she continued to hug me and stroke a hand up and down my arm.

The fatigue of being so magically drained started to pull me under again. "Sleepy," I informed her.

"Go to sleep, child, we'll keep you safe," she promised.

Triston tugged at our connection and I ignored it, imagining thick walls surrounding them. I imagined isolating them from the rest of me.

The hollowness expanded.

Large arms pulled me out of the SUV and carried me inside. “What’s wrong with her?” Rhys asked.

Ah, Rhys was carrying me.

“Take her to Kara,” Jolie said. “And speak softly.”

“Is Caleb—”

“He’s fine,” she said quickly.

Pain flared in my chest, and I whined.

“Best not to talk, Puff,” Jolie whispered, and it sounded like she had tears in her voice. Why was she sad?

Rhys set me on a cold table and soft hands ran along my body. “Ember, can you open your eyes?” Kara requested.

I tried, but they were so heavy. Trying again, I managed to get the heavy lids to crack open. “Heavy,” I breathed.

“Were you hit with a magic spell?” she asked.

“Magic. Drained.”

“Apparently, she created five portals while already pretty drained, shifted after that, and was fleeing before Kieran found her,” Nico said. “She fainted and is dealing with added emotional stress on top of that.”

Emotional stress? Yes, I supposed that was accurate.

“Alright, let’s get you a little relief,” Kara said.

Warmth spread from her hands slowly, starting to warm my freezing body.

“Where is she? What’s wrong?” Caleb asked, growling and angry.

I whimpered and tried to curl into a ball, but my body wasn't moving like I wanted it to.

"With me, now!" Jolie shouted.

"No, I—"

"That wasn't a request," she said and growled, sounding just like a dragon.

"Fox, help me," Kara snapped.

Another set of warm hands joined hers.

"I've never seen someone so magically depleted," Fox whispered.

So cold. I was still so cold.

Fur. Fur was warm.

Kara gasped. "She shifted? How can she shift with no magic?"

The blessed darkness took hold of me again and I fell asleep once more.

My stomach growled, but I didn't want to move. I was warm and comfortable. Though, my bladder did feel like it might explode.

Cracking one eye open, I found I was on my bed in Jolie's house. Opening both eyes and looking down, I realized I was still in rabbit form. Glancing around the room, my heart sank to find it empty.

My chest tightened again and my breaths became ragged.

Shaking my head, I clenched my eyes closed and slowed my breathing, taking big, deep breaths. Once able to breathe easier, I hopped to my bathroom and relieved myself. It was awkward in my rabbit form, but for a reason I couldn't explain, I didn't want to shift.

Hopping down the stairs proved harder, but I managed and made my way to the kitchen.

Deryn looked down when I headbutted the door open and his eyes widened. He caught the door before it swung back and hit me. "You're awake."

I bobbed my head and hopped towards the fridge. Looking up at it, I frowned as I realized I couldn't open the door. There were likely fruits and vegetables on the counter though. Hopping straight up, I cleared the countertop and managed to land on it.

"Please don't poop on the island," Deryn said.

I turned to look at him and rolled my eyes exaggeratedly.

He smirked, but it faded into a frown. "Why aren't you in human form?"

I shrugged and hopped over to the bowl of fruits and carefully pulled a few strawberries out.

Deryn pulled out a few more and set them next to the ones I had grabbed. "Everyone is out front."

Good, that meant I had time to eat and return to my room.

"They've been worried about you," he whispered.

I scoffed and kept eating my food.

"Mm, that explains the rabbit form." He finished the cup of whatever he was drinking and set it in the sink. "I'll let them know you're awake."

Finished eating the strawberries, I hopped off the counter and headed towards the door to go back to my room.

Just as I moved to headbutt it open, someone flung the door open, sending me flying backwards with a screech.

CHAPTER TWO

"Ember! I'm so sorry," Triston yelled and dropped down to pick me up, cradling me against his chest. "Are you okay? Did I hurt you?"

Yes, yesterday.

Struggling, I tried to get out of his hold, but he was rubbing his face against me, purring.

"We've been so worried. I thought you might never wake up. It's been two days."

Two days? Well, that explained the urgent need to use the restroom when I finally did wake up.

Finally able to get out of his hold, I headed for the door again.

"Where is she?" Branson demanded as he threw the door open to come inside, too, smacking me with the door and sending me head over tail with a pained screech.

"Shit, that's twice now," Triston groaned.

Branson scooped me up and twisted my body about as he inspected me. "Did I hurt you?"

I yelped at the movements, the spinning around making me dizzy.

He hugged me against his chest and sighed heavily. "You're okay."

"What's all this noise about?" Jolie asked. Her eyes widened when she saw me. "You're awake! It's about time, sleepyhead."

Trying to get out of Branson's hold was twice as hard as Triston's. He seemed to realize I wanted down and gently set me on the floor.

Triston immediately opened the door and held it open, which I was grateful for.

As I hopped towards the stairs, Caleb and Riddick walked in the front door.

Our eyes locked and we stared in silence for several heartbeats.

When they didn't move or speak, that pain in my chest returned, and I resumed my hopping up the stairs.

"We need to talk," Caleb said sternly.

I ignored him and continued hopping up the stairs. Hopping up was so much harder than hopping down. Why was that? Maybe I needed to see if we could alter the shape of the stairs at the new house to allow for easier upwards hopping.

"Ember," Caleb snapped, his alpha tone causing me to freeze.

"Please, talk to us," Riddick said and I heard Caleb grunt in pain. "Please shift and talk to us, Ember."

I stayed frozen, uncertain, but realized I couldn't hide from them forever, and it was childish to do so anyway.

Shifting, I stood and turned to face them, arms over my chest. "What?"

Caleb's eyes darted to my cheek and his jaw flexed as he clenched his teeth. "Scar."

"What?" I asked.

"You have a scar," he growled.

I did? What had I gotten a scar from?

Turning, I jogged up the stairs to my bathroom and looked in the mirror. He was right, I had a scar under my eye. It wasn't a normal scar though, and looked like it was the shape of a star.

"Not a scar," Riddick whispered, "a curse mark."

"What?" I gasped and spun around. "A curse mark?"

He nodded and reached out to touch it, but I backed away, bumping into my sink top. "Don't! What if it can transfer to you or something?"

"You already touched Triston and Branson," Caleb pointed out from in my room somewhere behind Riddick.

"That was in rabbit form before I realized I had it," I argued.

"So, what, you aren't going to touch us?" Caleb asked.

Riddick backed up so he was in my room and I could leave the bathroom.

Walking forward, I leaned against the doorjamb of my bathroom and asked, "Do you even want to touch me?" His arms were folded over his chest and he was glaring at me. "You look like you'd rather fight me than hug me."

"We've confirmed you can't have sense beaten into you at this point," he said and snarled.

"Get out," I whispered.

Riddick raised his hand. "Ember, wait, let's just talk and—"

"What do you want from me, Caleb? Do you want me to beg your forgiveness for saving your asses? To swear I would never do it again?"

"That would be a start," he snapped.

Riddick slapped a hand over his face. "Caleb, shut up."

"No, it's fine. I get it. You're mad at me. You're mad that I risked myself to save you. Well, guess what, Your Highness, I'll never apologize for that. And I would do it all again in a heartbeat. So, until you pull your head out of your ass, I don't want to see you."

"One more portal, Ember. You only had to make one more portal." His chest was heaving and his teeth were bared as he spoke.

"I almost killed myself making the ones I did!" I yelled.

"And yet you still won't admit you shouldn't have done it!" he shouted back.

"You would have done the same if you were in my shoes," I countered. "If you could have saved all of us and left yourself there to fight, you would have."

He opened his mouth and closed it.

Ha!

"You said you wouldn't shut me out or torment me like you did the last time you got mad at me," I reminded him. "Yet, neither of you has even *tried* to hug me or expressed your happiness that I'm alive and well after what we went through." After what I said ... though I wouldn't voice that part.

"We are happy you're well," Riddick said. "We're just also—"

"Assholes," I finished for him. Staring into Caleb's eyes, I put my hand over his mark on my wrist, and said, "I revoke your mark." A slight burn followed the words and his mark disappeared.

Caleb stumbled back, eyes wide in horror. "Em—"

Grabbing my phone, I waved it at him. "I'll be back in a few hours. See, advanced warning this time."

His eyes widened and Riddick reached for me as they both realized what I meant.

Unfortunately for them, I was fully recharged, so I teleported myself to my apartment. Once there, I went up to the roof, set my phone on the table, ignoring that it was already ringing, shifted into my rabbit form, and climbed into the planter box full of fluffy, leafy plants that hid me from the sun and made me feel safe.

The building shook and my eyes shot open. Was someone attacking the building again? How did they know I was here?

Hands reached into the leaves and grabbed me. I bit down, drawing blood.

"Ouch!" Caleb hissed as he finished pulling me out of my napping spot.

I'd started to feel bad for biting, but not when I realized it was him.

When I tried to wiggle my way out of his hands, he gently set me on the cushion of the loveseat and sat on the other cushion. "I don't blame you for biting me."

Hopping off the seat, I headed towards the door to go to my apartment.

"I'm sorry!" he shouted. "Can you please come back?"

Shifting forms, I shook my head at him. "No, you're not ready for me."

"I was never ready for you." He laughed softly. "You fell into my life and set it on fire."

I flinched and pressed a hand to my chest at the sudden pain. "Fuck you, Caleb."

He stepped in front of me, blocking my exit. "I didn't mean that in a bad way, Ember."

I stumbled back, remembering the curse mark. "Don't touch me. Not that you want to, anyway."

His eyes dropped to my wrist and he swallowed hard. "You teleported us, sent us away while you were left with hundreds of people determined to kill you. You said you didn't want to split the group and then forced us to leave. You teleported us so far away there was no hope of making it back to you. I sat there, waiting to feel your death, and when it didn't come, I didn't know what to do. Then Kieran flew to us and I saw you – alive, but barely, and all I could think about was how I had failed you. How I had almost let the woman I was courting die because I'm too weak and inexperienced. Because I let my concern for a stranger surpass my concern for you."

"You didn't fail anyone," I countered. "We're all alive and—"

He reached to grab my arms and I stumbled back and fell on my butt.

"You can't touch me! The curse mark—"

"Fuck the curse," he growled, pulled me up and kissed me deeply, his tongue stroking along mine and I moaned into his mouth. The warmth of him hugging me warmed up the void in my heart. He rested his forehead against mine and in a voice cracking with emotion whispered, "I love you, too, Ember. I love you more than anything in this world. I don't deserve you and that's why I was so mad. I am so sorry that I failed you."

Shaking my head slightly, I said, "You only failed me when you shut yourself away from me."

"Can you forgive me? Can you please give me a second chance to prove myself to you?"

"I love you, Caleb, but I'm still upset with you."

He nodded. "That's fair. I need to prove myself to you again."

"And now you're likely cursed just like I am," I whispered and choked on a sob. "What if we're both dying now?"

He wrapped his arms tighter around me. "Then we die together."

Leaning my head back, I captured his lips with mine and slid my hands along his waistband to push up beneath his shirt, and squeeze his back.

His kisses moved down my jaw, down my neck. He pulled me inside of the building, to his apartment, and laid me down on the couch. Leaning back, he yanked his shirt off and quickly unbuttoned and pulled his pants off.

I worked my shirt off and he removed my pants, immediately dropping down to suck and lick at my clit.

My hips arched up and I moaned, sliding my hands into his hair, I gripped him and ground myself against his mouth.

When my orgasm shattered me apart, my eyes unseeing as stars covered them, he pulled back only long enough to reposition himself and thrust into me.

"Ember," he gasped as he buried himself fully into me. "I don't want to be separated from you ever again." He arched back and thrust into me again, eyes fluttering closed. "The void in my soul hurts so much right now."

Wait ...

"You feel the hollowness, too?" I asked.

He stopped moving and opened his eyes. "Yes."

"But ... I can still feel our connection." I touched a hand to my chest.

He nodded. "Yes."

"So, what is that emptiness?"

Scowling, he thought about it a moment and said, "I don't know."

"Is it the mark being gone?" I asked and held up my wrist.

He flinched and said, "That could be it."

"But I felt it even before I revoked the mark," I whispered.

"You had already decided to do it, so I think it weakened the magic of it," he said softly.

"What do you mean I had already decided to do it?" I asked.

"At Leona's, I saw it in your eyes then, that you were debating it. You kept rubbing at your wrist. It was another reason I got so upset. And handled my emotions like a giant toddler."

"Will it go away if you mark me again?" I asked.

"I think so."

"Do you even *want* to mark me again?" Although we were in the process of making up, that didn't mean he wanted to go back to how things were. My voice was soft and I couldn't look into his eyes.

He tilted my chin up and stroked his finger across it. "I need to prove myself to you again. That's why you removed it, because you realized I wasn't capable of protecting you, of being the alpha you deserve."

His eyes darted to Branson's mark and widened. "You removed Branson's, too."

I didn't remember removing Branson's, but perhaps I had done it at the same time. "You all are a package deal, aren't you?"

"Let me prove myself to you," he begged. "Give me another chance?"

I looked down at our still joined bodies and said, "Pretty sure that's what's going on right now."

He smirked, leaned down to kiss me, and thrust back into me so hard and fast that he hit my cervix and that combination of pleasure and tiny bit of pain continued for the next few minutes until I orgasmed, and he orgasmed with me.

CHAPTER THREE

When we returned to the house, the other three crowded into my bed, taking any place they could, at my feet or head, just anywhere that they could touch me.

I slept surrounded by their touch and woke feeling refreshed.

That feeling was short-lived when I went to the bathroom and saw the curse mark had spread and was now a strange star symbol. Rushing out to the bedroom, my fears were confirmed when I saw the mark on all of the guys' faces as well.

"Fuck," I gasped. Grabbing my phone, I took a picture and sent it to Kara.

She texted back, "Looking into it."

"What's wrong?" Riddick asked as he rolled over and blinked sleep-filled eyes open.

"All of you have the curse mark now," I told him with a rough swallow.

"I already messaged Nana Kara," Caleb said, his voice muffled by the pillow his face was pressed into.

"Come back to bed," Triston said and reached a hand out for me.

"No, we need to get up," Caleb said, groaned, and rolled onto his back. "We have things to do today."

"What are we supposed to? Should we really go anywhere with a contagious curse mark?" It didn't seem like a good idea for us to go out around other people if we might give them the curse as well.

"We aren't going out around other people," Caleb said. He sat up and ran a hand through his hair. "Everyone, get ready and meet in the foyer. Don't touch my parents."

"How should we dress?" I asked.

"Jeans and a t-shirt," he answered, swung his leg out of bed, and shuffled to the door.

Triston and Branson followed him.

Riddick stood, wrapped his arms around me, and pulled me back onto the bed.

I yelped and then laughed as he cuddled me close.

"Five more minutes," he whispered and kissed my forehead.

"I think we can get away with five more minutes," I agreed, and wrapped my arms around him.

"Promise you're not mad at me anymore?" he asked softly.

"I won't lie and say I'm not still hurt," I whispered. "But the anger has gone."

He nodded. "We were pricks. I'm sorry. I swear that we'll make it up to you."

"Shh, you're interrupting my five minutes," I teased.

Squeezing me, he quieted and held me.

"What the shit?" Caleb demanded. "You two went back to sleep? Get up, you bums!" He hit us with pillows.

"Hey! Stop!" I shouted and put my hands up, trying to defend myself.

Riddick shifted into his cheetah form and pounced on Caleb, knocking him to the floor.

"Ember, help!" Caleb said and hit Riddick with the pillow. "I'm being mauled."

I folded my arms across my chest. "You started it by attacking me. Riddick is just being a good boyfriend and defending me."

Caleb knocked Riddick off and dove onto the bed, pinning me down. "Caught you!"

"I didn't try to run," I said, rolling my eyes.

"What the heck?" Triston asked from the doorway. "I thought we were leaving?"

"Right. Right," Caleb said and stood up, he pulled me to my feet and swatted my ass. "Get dressed."

I looked over my shoulder as I sauntered to the closet, sashaying my hips, and said, "Yes, alpha," in a deep voice.

He growled and took a step to come after me, heat in his eyes, but Triston and Riddick grabbed his arms and dragged him out. "Tease!" he shouted.

My phone dinged with a message, so I picked it up and my eyes widened when I saw the date on the lock screen. Our one year anniversary was in just a few days! Crap! Being asleep for several days had eaten up the time I should have had to finalize my plans.

The message was from Leona, asking if I was okay.

Sending her a quick message, I let her know that I was awake and feeling good.

Hurrying, I got changed, brushed my hair and teeth, and put on a little bit of eye makeup.

Satisfied, I ran down the stairs to the foyer. "I'm ready," I panted.

"Good, time to go," Caleb said and headed outside and to the garage. He tossed me my keys. "You're driving."

"Wait, we're going without a guard?" We never went anywhere without a guard.

"Yes," Caleb said with a nod.

Was that wise, considering they'd almost killed us just a few days ago?

"It'll be alright," Caleb reassured me.

Nodding, I climbed into the driver's seat and started the vehicle. It took me a minute to adjust the seat and mirrors to my liking before heading out.

"Where are we going?" I asked, glancing at him in the passenger's seat.

"I'll give you directions," he promised. "Head towards Leona's."

I hated not having advance notice or being unable to review the directions before going anywhere. Scowling, I accepted that he wanted to surprise me, and I was just going to have to go along with it.

Since I hated traffic, I took the longer route to drive around the city instead of through it, and no one complained.

Nearing Leona's, Caleb started to give me instructions on

which routes to take. An hour later, we were deep within a forest, and pulled up to a huge iron gate with a symbol I had never seen before.

There was a keypad next to me and Caleb had me punch in four numbers. The gate swung open and we drove down a bumpy, dirt path, the tall trees towering over us.

The trees opened to a large clearing where three buildings stood. Two of which were still heavily under construction, but the main building was finished and I knew exactly what it was when I saw it.

"Our house," I breathed and put the SUV in park. Climbing out, I stared at the house, the wrap around porch and balcony exactly as I had requested it.

The front door had that same symbol as the gate.

"Welcome to our new pack home!" Caleb said, his arms in the air as he walked backwards, a huge smile on his face.

"Whoa," Triston breathed, "it's huge."

Caleb pulled a set of keys out of his pocket and jingled them. "Ember, would you like to do the honors?"

I shook my head. "You're king, you should do it."

He walked up to me, forcing me to tilt my head back to see his face, and whispered, "What is a king without his queen?"

My heart thundered in my chest. "I, uh—"

Grabbing my hand, he gently set the keys in them, then spun around me, and pushed my lower back, ushering me to the front door.

I walked up the steps and ran my fingertips along the wood that still smelled freshly cut. To my right was the porch swing I had requested, and I felt tears in my eyes at the sight of it. There were two pillows on it, each with a rabbit outline.

Putting the key into the lock, I twisted it, and pushed open the door.

To the right was the sunken living room, two steps down, with a couch around the room and a huge rectangular cushion in the middle.

On the left was a dining table large enough to seat fifteen people. Straight ahead was the kitchen, large, full of brand-new appliances, and sparkling.

"It's perfect," I breathed.

"The only perfect thing about this place is you being here," Caleb whispered in my ear and pressed a soft kiss to my ear.

Romantic Caleb was definitely one of my favorites.

"Let's go look at the rooms," I suggested and started to head that way, but they all rushed in front of me to block me.

"You can't see the rooms yet," Riddick said.

"They're not ready," Branson added.

Okay, so they were clearly doing something to surprise me.

"Okay," I said and held up my hands, taking two steps back.

They relaxed and I used that distraction to try to run around them, but Triston snagged me around the waist, making me squeal.

"Not so fast, missy. I knew you'd backed down too quickly." He nipped at my ear and I chuckled.

"Foiled," I sighed. "What's the symbol on the gate and door?" I asked once he'd set me back on my feet.

"Our symbol," Caleb answered.

"Huh?"

"Every clan has a symbol," he explained. "Now that I'm taking on the mantle of King of the Hybrids, we needed a clan symbol."

Turning back towards the door, I walked up to inspect it. It was a combination of wolf for the werewolves, dragon wing for the dragon shifters, fire for the mages, tree for the elves, and musical notes for the sirens.

"It's beautiful," I whispered and stroked my fingers across the burned wood.

"Riddick designed it," Caleb said.

"You did a great job," I praised and turned to give him a smile, smiling wider when I saw the red on the tips of his ears.

"Speaking of you taking on the mantle, is there going to be a ceremony?" Branson asked. "Don't you always hold a ceremony for a new crowning?"

"Each clan holds their own, but since we don't have our clan fully formed yet, we won't hold one," Caleb said and I could not only see the sadness in his eyes, but hear it in his voice.

"No," I said immediately. "No, we're going to have a ceremony. It doesn't matter how small our clan is, we are going to crown you."

"It's not necessary," Caleb said.

"On the contrary, it's more than necessary, it's required," Triston said. "Ember is right, as our king, you are going to get the whole thing."

"Our clan no longer consists of just the five of us," Branson reminded him. "We have other members now."

"And it will send a message to all hybrids out there, to let them know we are here and welcome them to join us," Branson said. "We can have pictures from it sent to the news outlets and post on our socials as well."

"Well, it's going to have to wait until we figure out this curse mark," Caleb reminded us.

I flinched. "Sorry."

All turned to me.

"Why are you apologizing?" Branson asked.

"Because I'm the one who got it and spread it to you all."

"You didn't ask to be cursed, Ember. You can't think it's your fault." Riddick shook his head. "The fault is on the one who cursed you to begin with."

"Are we here to isolate ourselves?" I asked. "That will be hard to do without me going to the bedroom."

"We are going to sleep in the living room," Riddick answered.

"Wait, we really are staying the night here?" I asked, looking around at them.

Caleb nodded. "We brought food since the pantry and fridge aren't stocked yet."

"Oh." How was I going to finalize my anniversary plans now? I was still debating how I wanted to handle the delivery of the mating stones.

"You sound disappointed," Branson commented.

"No, I just had a few things to do at the house." I still had a couple of days. "It will be nice to spend our first night together here."

"Let's carry in the supplies," Caleb said and headed out the front door.

Branson and Triston followed, but Riddick stayed with me.

"Ember, I know you and I haven't had much time alone and I know things have been ... insane, but I wanted to tell you how sorry I am about how we treated you after the battle. It's been weighing on my mind ever since and I know a simple apology won't fix things, but I really am sorry."

He did look like a man tormented. Reaching out, I gripped his hand and asked, "Do you love me, Riddick?"

His hand squeezed mine and he reached out to grab my other hand. "I do."

"Promise me something?"

"Anything."

"If this curse kills me, don't let Caleb shy away from becoming king still. I feel in my soul that this is what he's supposed to do."

"You're not going to die, Ember," he said sternly and pulled me into chest, hugging me tightly. "We're going to find a way to break the curse and enjoy our anniversary."

"So, you guys do remember our anniversary?" I teased.

He pushed me back and asked, "How could I forget the day the most beautiful woman in the world tossed the mage king across her lawn?"

Laughing, I shook my head. "That feels like it was a lifetime ago."

Fingertips brushing my cheek, he smiled and said, "It's been the best lifetime I've ever experienced."

Going up on my toes, I pressed a kiss to his cheek. "Thank you."

"Riddick makes breakfast since he didn't help carry supplies in," Caleb ordered.

Riddick winked at me and said, "Worth it."

CHAPTER
FOUR

Just as we were finishing our lunch of sandwiches and salads, Caleb's phone rang. He set it on the center of the dining room table we all sat at and answered it on speaker phone. "Nana, you're on speaker. Did you find something?"

"Where are you right now?" she demanded.

"Our clan house," he answered. "We thought isolating ourselves would be smart, to avoid infecting my parents."

"Who was the first one to get the mark and when?" she asked and it sounded like she was walking somewhere outdoors.

"Ember, and the day we were in that huge fight at the park, three days' ago," Riddick answered.

"Shit," she hissed. "Can you teleport here?"

"Ember has never been there, so she can't teleport there. Nana, what's going on?"

"I need you to get Ember to me as soon as possible. Can you teleport to your parents' house?"

I nodded. "I can."

"Teleport to the front yard, bring all of you. When you get there, do not touch anyone. Wait for me."

"We understand," Caleb said and hung up. "Clean up fast and then we'll teleport."

My heart hammered in my chest as I stood on shaky legs to carry my plate to the kitchen. Why was Kara, Queen of the Elves and one of the best healers in the world, so scared?

Triston took my plate from me and I was left standing in the open area of the kitchen, watching them.

They hurried back to me and set their hands on me.

Taking a deep breath, I envisioned the grassy area where we practiced fighting at Caleb's parents' house and teleported us there.

When I opened my eyes, I was shocked to find Dan, Emrys, and his parents outside.

Jolie took a step towards us, but Deryn grabbed her and stopped her. Tears filled her eyes. "Ember, how are you feeling?"

Scowling, I said, "I feel great. What's wrong? What's going on?"

A white sedan raced down the drive, up to the house, and skidded to a stop. As soon as it stopped, Kara jumped out of the passenger side and walked quickly towards us.

"Kara, what's going on?" I asked, my heart pounding still.

"I need you to do something that you won't like," she informed me.

"What?" Caleb asked, growling softly.

"You have to sever the connection you have with them," she said and swallowed hard. "It's going to hurt and you're immediately going to feel the curse come back to you and that's going to hurt even worse."

"What?" I gasped. Sever our connection? I didn't even know that was possible. Plus ... what would happen once it was severed?

"Nana, there has to be another way," Caleb said, his chest heaving and eyes darting towards me.

"She's killing you all by sharing the curse with you. The only reason she's not dead yet is because you're sharing it with her and your shared powers are keeping her alive!" Kara yelled.

I gasped. "How do I sever the connection?"

"Ember," Riddick pleaded.

"I'm not going to let you die."

"You're going to sacrifice yourself again?" Caleb snapped.

"She's not going to die, Caleb. I'm going to break the curse once it's back on her," Kara said and smiled reassuringly at him.

"Why can't you break it now?" Riddick asked.

"Because it's spread between you all and it's not possible to break like that. Please, Ember, we don't have much time. Take this, and cut your bonds." She tossed a knife towards me that had strange symbols on it.

Jolie gasped and stumbled backwards, hands at her chest.

Her mates swarmed around her, blocking her sight and consoling her.

Caleb growled loudly. "No. No! There has to be another way."

"There isn't. Besides, you'll still be able to form a mate bond," Dan said as he tried to soothe Caleb.

Turning to face him, I smiled and said, "Well, I guess we'll find out once and for all if you are with me for the connection or not."

My attempt at levity fell flat as all four of the men growled.

"It's going to hurt you four as well," Emrys advised them. "And you can't touch her until after Kara removes the curse."

"Ember," Branson whined.

"How?" I asked Kara.

"Look at your chest, you should be able to feel the bonds there. Grasp one, and cut it with the knife."

Jolie sobbed and dropped to her knees.

"Mom! Go inside!" Caleb shouted. "You don't need to witness this."

Rhys picked her up and carried her inside of the house.

"I'm sorry," Fox said, tears in his eyes. "I'm so sorry, Caleb. It's going to hurt so much. You're going to feel like a piece of you died. I'm so sorry." He turned and ran into the house after the others, slamming the door closed behind him.

Katar, Emrys, and Dan moved closer, but still not close enough they might touch us.

Another vehicle raced down the street and out of this one poured Leona and her mates. "We're here!" Leona called.

"Perfect timing," Kara said. "Are you sure you can calm them down?"

"I don't know about Caleb, but I should be able to calm the others, since they don't have siren blood," she said.

Looking at me, tears filled her eyes. "I'm sorry, sirenling. You're going to experience it all without my help or anyone else's. It's going to hurt a lot, so you need to be ready."

Now I was completely terrified. How bad was this pain going to be?

"Hurry, Ember," Kara urged me. "I don't know how quickly things will progress to a point that I won't be able to break it."

Nodding, I looked down at my chest and reached with the hand not holding the knife. It gripped one of the connections, Triston's. I met his eyes and smiled.

"I love you," he whispered.

My eyes widened, it was the first time he'd said it to me, but I didn't have time to enjoy it. I had to do this before they all died. I sliced the knife through the invisible bond. The bond was anything but insubstantial. The instant it severed, it felt like I'd cut one of my arms off. My head fell back and I screamed.

Triston roared and fell to his knees, clutching at his chest, tears falling down his face.

Leona started singing and his sobs quieted, but didn't stop.

Pain tore into my body, a sizzling, burning pain like lava through my veins. I gasped and staggered.

"Again, Ember," Kara whispered.

I grasped another bond, Branson's.

"I've always loved you, Ember. Ever since I woke up in your cabin," he whispered.

Tears in my eyes, I sliced through it.

Screaming, I fell to my knees, panting and seeing stares as the sizzling in my veins grew.

"Ember!" Caleb shouted.

"Two more, Ember," Kara said soothingly. "I'm sorry. Just two more."

My bonds with Riddick and Caleb were stronger than the others', so I was terrified what it would feel like to sever them.

"I ... can't," I cried. "It hurts too much."

"You have to," she said. "Or severing the other two will be for nothing and you three will die."

Sobbing, I sat back on my heels, reached a shaking hand up and grasped one of the last two, Riddick's.

He whined and I gave him a shaky smile, trying to use humor to ease us both into it, and said, "Sorry, gorgeous. Doctor's orders."

The knife cut through it easily, which was good since I had no energy.

Riddick and I screamed simultaneously, and he fell onto his side, curled into a ball. My pain escalated threefold and I saw black around the edges of my vision.

I had to do it before I fainted. I grasped the connection and my arms shook.

"Ember," Caleb whined, "wait."

"Can't," I panted. "Hurts so much. Lava in veins."

"That's the curse. Shit. Hurry, Ember. Cut it," Kara shouted.

"Sorry, my king. I have to disobey your orders," I whispered. Before he could respond, I cut through our bond.

Caleb's head jerked back and he roared so loudly that it shook the ground.

A hole had formed in my chest and I simultaneously felt numb in my core and like acid had been poured into my heart and was being pumped throughout my body.

I fell onto the ground and my body started seizing, eyes rolled up into the back of my head.

"Hurry, Kara!" Katar shouted.

Someone was growling and roaring, hissing and spitting, and several people were shouting.

It was too much. Too much pain. Too empty. Too numb. Too hot. Too ... dead.

CHAPTER FIVE

"She should have woken up by now," Kara whispered near me. "Did I do it wrong? Did I just kill my grandson's potential mate?"

"She's breathing, Mom, so she's not dead," Silverowl said softly.

"How are they doing?" she asked, her voice moving around me in a circle.

"Despondent. They're only eating because we're using alpha orders to force them. They're just sitting in her room, silently staring at nothing," Leona replied.

Why was it so hard to move my body? My eyes didn't want to open. Everything felt so heavy and unmovable.

Trying to open my mouth to speak didn't work either. Could I whine?

A strange squeak was the only sound made.

"Did you hear that?" Leona asked.

"Ember?" Silverowl whispered. "Ember, can you hear me?"

Trying again, I was finally able to move a finger.

"She twitched!" Leona gasped.

"Thank goodness," Kara sighed.

"Let's try warming her up," Silverowl suggested. "Maybe her muscles are too cold."

Warm, heavy blankets draped over me and I felt a little better.

An hour later, I was finally able to crack my eyes open.

"There she is," Kara said with a smile. "Welcome back, Rubyhare. We've missed you."

"Curse?" I asked, my voice rough from lack of use.

Silverowl held a cup of water with a straw up so I could drink from it. "Mom broke it. You five are all clear."

Clear, but no longer connected.

"Day?" I asked after finishing my drink, my throat soothed a bit from the cool liquid.

"It's the day before your anniversary," Leona answered.

"Come on, let's get you to the dining room to eat," Silverowl said.

I shook my head. "Not hungry."

"It wasn't a request, sweetheart," he said and picked me up.

Jolie gasped and ran over to us as Silverowl carried me into the dining room and set me in a chair. "Ember! You're awake, oh, sweetheart."

Tears filled my eyes, but Silverowl gently moved her to the side. "She needs to eat, Jolie."

Jolie stood, turned, and started making a plate of food for me.

Dan got to his feet, walked over, and dropped to a knee

beside me. "I owe you a debt, Ember. Whatever you want, whenever, just ask me. Okay?"

Why? Why did he think I was owed anything?

He patted my hand, stood, and walked back to his seat.

"Eat," Jolie ordered me and set the plate of food before me. Eggs, bacon, sausage, pancakes, a waffle, and hash browns.

So, it was morning time.

I tried to lift my arm, to grab my fork, but it was hard. My brows furrowed as I tried again and slowly, my arm rose, shaking so hard that I knew I wouldn't be able to hold a fork.

"It's okay," Silverowl whispered beside me, squatting down next to my chair. "It's going to take your body just a bit to reacclimate is all."

Reacclimate? It was like I had to learn to live again. He sounded confident it would happen. The hole in my chest begged to differ.

"Ember?" Riddick asked softly.

I turned my head slowly, my eyes landing on Riddick and Caleb, both pale and hunched in on themselves.

Caleb raised his head and when our eyes met, the space in my chest throbbed. He raced towards me, shoved Silverowl out of the way, and picked my hands up, pressing kisses along my knuckles. "You're awake. Are you okay?" he reached out and pressed a hand to my cheek.

"She's still a little out of it," Silverowl informed him.

Caleb turned slightly towards Silverowl and growled. Turning back to me, he wiped tears from my face I hadn't realized had fallen. "Can you talk? What's wrong?"

"It's gone," I whispered. "I'm ... empty. A shell."

He flinched and nodded. "I know, sweetheart. I know. I ... we feel the same."

"Did ... did it work?" I asked.

"Yes," he said and nodded. "The curse is gone and we're all safe."

At least I had accomplished that.

"N-Now what?" I asked, my teeth chattering as I started to feel cold again.

Silverowl started to bring me a blanket, but after a warning growl from Caleb, he handed it to Caleb instead.

Caleb draped it around my shoulders, and rubbed my arms over the blanket. "Now, we get you to eat some breakfast, and take a nice, long bath. What happens after that can be figured out then."

"And do you ..." My eyes darted to our audience, and I stopped my question. I didn't want to ask him that with everyone here.

"Do I what, Ember?" he asked as he continued to rub my arms.

"Do you think you can help me eat?" I asked. Raising my shaking arm again, I showed that I wasn't yet able to use the fork.

He smiled, one of his blindingly charming, handsome smiles, and said, "Anything for you, my queen."

The statement, so full of love and caring, broke me. Throwing myself out of the chair and against his chest, I sobbed so loudly I worried I might break his eardrums.

He caught me and lifted me easily into his arms. "Riddick, grab her food. Nana, do you need to check her again or can we take her upstairs?"

"You can take her. She needs warmth and emotional support now."

"I know, Nana. We all do," Caleb said and nuzzled my ear. "I've got you, Emmy."

With my head rested on his shoulder, I drew in deep breaths of his scent, letting it fill my lungs.

"We've been so worried," he whispered in my ear. "Nana thought you would wake up just a few hours after the curse broke. We've been anxiously waiting for you to wake up."

"How do you feel?" I asked. "They said you were despondent."

"We were terrified we were going to lose you, Emmy. Of course we were." His hold on me tightened. "I can't imagine how painful that was for you to go through four times. Just once almost destroyed each of us. I got into a fight with both Papa Dan and Emrys. Auntie Leona had to put us all to sleep."

"How does it feel?" I asked. "Are you ..."

"Empty?" he asked and nodded. "Yes."

"Cold," Riddick said behind us.

"Worried," Triston said from the bedroom doorway. He smiled and tears built in his eyes. "Hello, sleepy girl. We've been waiting for you."

"She's awake?" Branson shouted from the room and came thundering towards us.

"Shush, you're too loud," Caleb chastised him.

"Sorry," Branson whispered and smiled at me. "Hello, beautiful."

Caleb sat down with his back against the headboard of my bed, set me between his legs, and wrapped the blanket tighter around me, with his arms around me on top of the blanket.

Riddick sat in front of me, stabbed some eggs onto the fork, and held it out for me to eat. "Come on, you've got to eat."

Caleb whispered in my ear in a deep, husky voice, "Be a good girl and eat."

A bit of warmth blossomed within me, but I was still too weak, too numb and cold to do more than open my mouth and obey.

"Good girl." The words were a soft growl that raised the hair on my arms.

They were acting like nothing had happened. Like our bonds weren't gone, destroyed, never to be reformed.

Riddick continued to feed me and I continued to eat.

When I started crying, no one asked me what was wrong or complained. They just continued to feed me and Caleb continued to hold me.

As soon as I finished the last piece, Branson took me from Caleb, letting the blanket fall, and carried me to the bathroom where a steaming tub full of water waited for me.

He set me on the sink counter, pulled my shirt off over my head, helped me stand, keeping an arm around my waist, and Triston pulled the pajama pants I was wearing off.

Immediately, I started shaking and my teeth started chattering together.

Branson picked me up and quickly lowered me into the tub.

Triston and he worked together to pour the hot water over my head, avoiding getting it on my face.

Both knelt beside the tub, watching and keeping an eye on me as I soaked.

"Is it hot enough?" Triston asked.

I nodded and my eyes widened at the ability to perform the movement. "Yes, thank you."

They went silent again and dropped their eyes to their hands in their laps. Were they trying to give me a semblance of privacy?

When my skin started to prune, I wiggled my feet, raised my arms, and moved my legs, happy to see I was finally able to move normally. "So much better," I whispered.

"Are you ready to get out?" Branson asked.

I nodded.

Triston grabbed a towel and waited while Branson picked me up by my armpits.

"I can stand," I said, but didn't fight him.

Once on my feet, Triston and he each used a towel to dry me down. Riddick walked in with a new pair of pajamas, including a pair of fluffy socks. I put everything on, then slowly walked to the sink to brush my teeth.

All three hovered, like they were worried I might fall over at any moment.

Turning around, I gave them a small smile. "I feel much better, thank you."

They all nodded and stepped out of my way so I could exit the bathroom.

Caleb sat on the edge of the bed, playing with the fork. He raised his eyes and smiled at me. "You look better. Much less pale."

Standing in the center of them, circled around me, I

finally asked the question I needed to know. "Has this changed us?"

Riddick's head canted slightly. "Physically? Yes. The bond we had is gone."

I shook my head, my breath shuddering as I exhaled. "Us. Us."

Triston reached out and gently took my hand. "Darling, are you asking if our feelings have changed?"

"If our relationship has changed?" Branson asked.

I nodded, unable to look at them, staring instead at their bare feet.

"Our love for you isn't from the bond," Branson said and hugged me from behind. "I've loved you since I woke up in your tiny cabin and you barely batted an eye at a bear trying to maul you."

"Sweetheart," Caleb whispered and dropped down into a crouch in front of me so I had to look at his face, "is this what you've been worried about since you saw me? What you wanted to ask earlier?"

Tears were sliding down my face as I nodded.

He straightened, cupped my face between his hands, and gently kissed my lips. "Our feelings for you haven't changed. If anything, they've grown stronger understanding how much you endured to save us from the curse. What you are willing to do for us." Kissing me again, he whispered against my lips, "And I vow to do everything in my power to never let that happen again. To keep you from experiencing pain ever again."

"We all love you, Ember," Triston said. "Even if we hadn't said so before and were being stubborn."

Branson grunted. “Emotions are hard, but I know for certain that I love you, Ember. Always have and always will.”

“Come on,” Riddick coaxed and pulled me towards the bed, “we need a cuddle puddle.”

They loved me. All four of them.

CHAPTER SIX

Four hours of cuddling, being fed lunch, and four more hours of cuddling later, I finally felt a little closer to normal.

Jolie told me the hole in my chest, the numbness there, would not disappear until we formed mating bonds. At least that had been her experience.

Luckily for me, today was our anniversary. So, if things went according to plan, I would be mated to them by this evening.

Since the H.E. was still at large, we opted to hold our anniversary celebration at our pack house instead of risking going out in public.

Nico and the guys had spent half the day creating and reinforcing wards around our land and the house specifically.

I spent the day getting the bloodstones from Leona's, getting my hair and makeup done, and trying to stop freaking out.

Shaking my hands out, I paced around in my room, watching the clock and counting down the minutes until I would leave.

Ezio was picking me up and driving me to the pack house since the guys were there, preparing things.

Looking back at the mirror, I admired the red dress Leona had given me for my birthday. It hugged my curves, was lowcut down the front to show off my cleavage, and had an open back.

Jolie had given me a diamond necklace that was a long chain of diamonds and hung down the center of my chest, which added a bit of sparkle to the outfit. I had spent an hour curling my hair and pinning the front back so it wouldn't fall into my face. My makeup was pretty simple, since I wasn't very good at it yet, but I'd added eyeliner, red eyeshadow, and mascara.

I had opted for low red heels since we wouldn't be walking much and I could take them off at any time while we were in the house.

Grabbing the black velvet box, I inspected the bloodstones. They were clear crystal gems the size of a grain of rice each. They would put a bit of their power and a drop of blood into each one and I would then place against my skin and they would permanently embed there. Jolie had combined two of her mates into one, so she only had two bloodstones, but I wasn't going to try that since hybrids were unknown and we didn't know if that would make them explode or not, something she'd dealt with. So, I would place them into a diamond shape on one side of my face. Leona had suggested two under each eye, but I liked how they looked in a diamond shape on the one side. I had already put some of my power and a drop of blood onto four bloodstones that the guys would put on themselves for me as well, but I wasn't sure where they would place them, as that was their decision. Some put them on their wrist, behind their ears, or on their face.

I had four boxes, each with two bloodstones, one for me and one for them, and the plan was to have them open the boxes simultaneously.

A horn honked outside, letting me know Ezio was here. Taking a deep breath, I grabbed the bag with the gifts and my change of clothes, grabbed the side of my dress, and walked down the stairs to the foyer.

Jolie, Deryn, Fox, Rhys, and Nico were in the living room playing videogames. When I walked by, Jolie whistled and all turned to look at me. "Do a spin," she ordered and made a circle with her finger.

I did a spin, and they all clapped.

"You have all the items you need?" she asked, knowing my plan for tonight.

I held up my bag. "All in here."

"Okay, one more thing," she said.

"Okay?" What else could there be?

"Take a deep breath and relax. You're going to see your boyfriends, not a firing squad." She smiled wide, and it gave me the break in tension I needed.

My shoulders relaxed as I laughed. "Thank you. Wish me luck!"

"You don't need luck," she said and shook her head. "Have fun!"

Ezio waited beside the passenger door, and when I walked out, he opened it for me and bowed. "Good evening."

"Hello, Ezio. Thanks for driving me." I tried to climb up into the SUV, but the dress made it a bit difficult.

He scooped me up and set me on the seat, tucking my dress inside carefully to avoid soiling it or it getting stuck in the door. "You are welcome. Beats hunting people down or being on babysitting duty."

Once he climbed in, I turned and asked, "Why aren't you mated? You can't tell me there aren't women at your door constantly." He was very handsome, kind, and a powerful alpha.

He shrugged. "Just wasn't in the cards for me, it seems. I've had several girlfriends, was in love twice, but neither time worked out." Glancing over at me as we drove, he said, "For what it's worth, I can tell you beyond a shadow of a doubt that those four love you. I know things have been rough lately, especially with Caleb, but being an alpha makes love more difficult than it does for non-alphas."

"How so?" I asked, curious.

"An alpha's job is to protect. It sings through our veins and minds constantly. So, when someone gets hurt on our watch, it upsets us, but when someone we love gets hurt, it's a stab to our soul. When Caleb was a child, I failed to protect him. Thankfully, he wasn't injured. That talented brat actually kept me safe that day, but that failure ate at me for years. It still does sometimes, to be honest, and is part of why I don't mind being on guard duty for you all. I heard about what you did when you were trapped, how you rescued them and sacrificed yourself. I won't say whether what you did was right or wrong, but it reminded me of Jolie. She put herself in danger a few times and it ate at the princes. When Jolie's bonds were cut, I was there with the princes. I saw the fear, the pain, the sheer panic in them as the one they were meant to protect was hurt. I know you all went through something similar recently."

I nodded and clutched at my chest.

"My point in all this is to say that I can tell you five are meant for each other, but being meant for each other and it being easy ain't the same thing. You've been through a lot this year and so have they. You've all also grown a lot this year. I'm excited to see where you all go from here. You are a very special woman, Rubyhare Ember."

I blinked rapidly and looked up at the roof of the car. "You're going to make me cry, Ezio."

He chuckled. "Okay, I'll stop being the sentimental old man now."

"Thank you," I whispered. "For everything you've said. There are still so many things I don't understand about the shifter communities, how you act and think, and how alphas are different than others."

"You'll get used to it eventually. Look at Jolie. She was once viewed as a strange human woman and now she's one of the most integral members of our societies. I think you'll be just as vital once you fully find your place."

I sighed and leaned my elbow on the door. "You mean as a queen? Acorns, it's weird to say out loud."

He laughed. "One day at a time, right? That's the only way any of us can handle these chaotic lives among royalty."

Joining his laugh, I nodded. That was for sure.

At the gate, he punched in the code and drove us up to the house. Once there, he opened the door and helped me get out, then winked and said, “Go get ‘em, Ember.”

“Thanks, Ezio.”

He nodded and drove away.

Taking a deep breath, I looked up at the house ... our house ... and squared my shoulders. Time for my first ever anniversary celebration.

Man, that made me sound so pathetic.

Snorting at myself, I walked up the steps and tried the door, but it was locked.

“What?” I didn’t have a key on me.

I knocked twice, and the door was pulled open.

Triston smiled down at me, wearing a nice midnight blue silk button-up shirt. “Good evening, beautiful.”

CHAPTER SEVEN

"Hello, handsome," I breathed, his scent blowing through the door and into my nose and making me inhale deeper.

He stepped back to let me inside, and I gasped at the transformed room. Candles, silver streamers, and flowers changed it into a stunning and warm room.

Branson stepped away from the dining table where he'd been adjusting silverware, and bowed to me. "Welcome home."

"Can I take your bag?" Triston asked.

Jerking it to my chest, I shook my head. "I have gifts inside."

His lip twitched, but he just bowed and waved me towards the living room. "If you'll take a seat, we will bring refreshments and hors d'oeuvres shortly."

Carefully, I walked down the two steps to the living room, set my bag in the corner out of the way, and sat on the edge of one of the couches. The house was so quiet, so peaceful, the forest through the windows the same. I definitely looked forward to living here.

Riddick stepped into the room, black slacks and a black shirt with the sleeves rolled up, his hair slicked back, and a tray of sparkling wine glasses. "Would you care for a drink, my lady?"

Smiling, I carefully took one off the tray. "Thank you. You look handsome tonight."

He set the tray in the center of the rectangular cushion, took my free hand, dropped to one knee, and pressed a kiss to my knuckles. "You are stunning, a goddess among us mere mortals. Your dress only accentuates your perfection and that color suits you well, Rubyhare."

My face was on fire. These sweet-talking men would be the death of me. "Thank you."

He brushed another kiss across my knuckles and stood. "Please excuse me. I'll return shortly."

When they'd said we would have dinner here, I hadn't expected them to serve me like this. Not that I was complaining.

"For our hors d'oeuvres this evening, we have a cheese croustade, mini deviled crab cornbread muffins, smoked salmon with caviar and prosciutto, and cucumber sandwiches." Caleb set two trays of delicious looking foods on the cushion on either side of the tray of drinks, and dropped to a knee before me. "Thank you for joining us this evening, little goddess."

My lip twitched, but I didn't let the full smile show. "Were you expecting someone else?"

His lip twitched and he let it grow into a full smile. "I

only ever wish for you to be near me, my queen." Leaning forward, he pressed a kiss to my cheek, whispered in my ear, "You look positively *delectable*."

My flush went down into my neck. "As do you, my king."

He growled softly and nuzzled my neck. "Two words and my resolve disappears," he whispered.

"Tsk, bad alpha! Bad!" Triston hissed.

My laughter was cut short as Caleb nipped my neck before straightening and backing up so I could see all of them seated on the couch across from me.

After taking a drink to calm my racing pulse, I picked up one of the cheese croustades and popped it into my mouth. I moaned. "So good."

Caleb closed his eyes and took a deep breath before counting to five quietly.

My lips quirked up into a smile, and I grabbed a different snack. The crab cornbread muffin. "So good," I breathed.

"Stop, you naughty vixen," Triston accused and shook his head.

"Sorry," I said and laughed. "I couldn't help it. These are *really* good though. Where did you order them from?"

"We didn't order anything, except the wine," Riddick answered.

"You guys made all this?" I asked, looking at the fancy items before me.

They all nodded.

"Well, they made it," Caleb amended. "I just helped plate it all."

"I'm incredibly impressed," I told them.

"Wait until you see the main course," Branson said with a wink.

As I ate another item, a cucumber sandwich, I enjoyed the view before me. The four of them were all dressed nicely, slacks and button-up shirts, and hair styled. Though all four were barefoot, but that made sense as they were inside of the house.

Caleb picked up a glass of wine and the others followed suit. He raised it and said, "A toast."

I raised my glass.

"To our first year and the many more to come," he said.

"Cheers!" I said, and we all tapped the edge of our glasses against each other's before drinking.

"Are you ready for dinner?" Riddick asked.

"Yes, please," I said, but looked down at the hors d'oeuvres longingly.

"We'll keep these for snacks later and can store them to eat tomorrow as well," Triston said when he noticed.

Branson hurried over to me and offered me his bent arm. "Shall we?"

I stood, slid my arm through his, and nodded. "We shall."

He smiled, and I felt it warm a little part of my core that had been cold before. Slowly, he led me to the table and pulled out my chair for me at the head of the table. I sat, and he pushed the chair in before taking a seat at the table.

Caleb sat at the other end, taking the head chair. Branson and Triston sat on the left while Riddick sat on the right after putting our drinks on the table before each of us.

Before us was a steamy, juicy looking roast, potatoes

with herbs, salad, and … a single large carrot right in front of my plate.

Caleb's smile grew when he saw me look at it. All four of them tensed, waiting for my reaction.

Picking it up, I inspected it, then bit a chunk off and ate it. "Pretty sweet," I commented.

The four males burst into laughter.

"Thank you," Triston said and wiped at his eyes. "That was perfect."

"Now, let's eat!" Caleb shouted.

Taking my plate, they passed it around to fill with food, each putting something on it before passing it back and setting it before me.

I waited until they'd all made their plates before I started eating. It was all phenomenal. Cooked so everything was tender, juicy, and sweet.

I ate until I couldn't fit anymore into my stomach and sighed contentedly. "That was the best meal I've had in a very long time," I praised.

"We're glad you liked it," Caleb said. "Now, it's time for presents. Let's move to the living room. Riddick, will you refresh the drinks?"

Caleb walked over to me, pulled out my chair, and offered me his arm.

"Is it alright with everyone if I give you my gifts first?" I asked as we walked back to the kitchen. "I'd like you to all open them at the same time."

"Of course," he said with a nod. "Whatever you'd like, Emmy."

I stopped at the stairs to the living room, realizing I

didn't have nicknames for Caleb, Triston, or Caleb. "My king," didn't count. Did that make me a terrible girlfriend?

"Ember?" Caleb asked, frowning. "Is something wrong?"

"No," I said and smiled up at him. "Just got caught in a thought."

"They can be sticky," he said with a wink.

Scoffing and shaking my head, I took the two steps down and walked over to my bag, taking out the four boxes.

The guys took the same spot on the one couch, newly filled wine on the cushion. Turning, I gave them my brightest smile and instructed, "Don't open until I say." Then, set a box in each of their hands. Stepping back so I could see them all, I said, "Okay, open them."

They opened the boxes and silently stared at them, eyes widened, but no words.

"I know things have been a bit crazy lately, but this is something I've been planning and now that the curse is gone, and we are moving into our pack house, I wanted to make my intentions clear. I would be honored if you would allow me to become your mate."

The speech wasn't nearly as much as I had practiced or wanted to say, but their shocked faces, still bodies, had me nervous that they weren't going to accept.

Caleb was the first to react. Tilting his head back, he let out a loud, laugh.

The laugh caught me off guard and I took a flinching step back, my face falling and tears threatening.

Was I wrong? Did they not want to be with me?

Had I misunderstood everything they said? No, I couldn't be wrong. Everyone couldn't be wrong!

I turned, preparing to teleport myself away, but Caleb grabbed my wrist and gently turned me, smiling down at me. "I'm sorry for laughing, Ember, but ... well, look." He tilted his head towards the cushion and the guys.

Looking over, I watched as they each pulled a small black box out of their pockets, opening them to reveal bloodstones.

Caleb pulled one out of his pocket, opened it, and dropped to one knee before me. "Rubyhare Ember Jasperwood, will you do us the honor of becoming our mate, our partner, our queen?"

I smacked his shoulder and growled. "You ass! I thought you were upset by my gift."

"Only because you beat us to it and ruined the surprise we'd been working on for weeks!" he said and wiggled the box at me. "So, what do you say?" One of the bloodstones inside of his box glowed, which meant he'd already put his power and blood into it.

"I say, we have eight bloodstones to sell." Chuckling, I wiped the now happy tears from my face, threw my arms around him, and kissed him. "Yes. Always yes."

CHAPTER
EIGHT

Jolie had warned me that to be fully mated, each race required a different thing. Mages and elves each used a spell. Dragons and wolves used a bite. With us being hybrids, we weren't sure which was going to be required. So, they had researched information for all options.

"Which are we going to try first?" I asked. The guys had all opted to put the bloodstone from me beneath their right eye. So, I had put the four bloodstones in the diamond formation beneath my right eye as well.

"We're going to try biting, since that's the easiest," Caleb answered.

"First, we need a picture," Triston said as he set his phone on the windowsill and put a book in front of it so it would stay standing upright.

"A picture?" I asked as I stood off the couch.

"Look at you, we need this gorgeous dress documented." I smiled, and he added, "Plus, I thought you might like to have a picture of us on our anniversary with our fresh bloodstones."

"I would," I said with a nod. I loved how considerate he was.

"Line up," he ordered us.

Caleb stood at my right, Riddick on my left, Branson on Caleb's left and Triston on Riddick's left. We all turned so our right side faced the camera.

Triston stepped forward, and said, "Three second delay ... now!" He pressed the button and stepped back into position. "Smile!"

There was no way I would stop smiling at this rate. The camera flashed and Triston checked the picture. "Looks good to me." He held out the phone. "What do you think?"

I looked down at the picture and nodded, smiling wider. "It's perfect." I was going to print it and put it in my room.

"Great, now we can get you out of that dress," Caleb said, his hand dropped down to my lower back and he reached up, releasing the clip that held the halter top. The dress fell and pooled down at my feet, exposing the matching lace thong I was wearing.

Riddick groaned. "Fuck, that's hot."

Caleb cupped my cheek and rubbed his thumb over the bone. "The bite's going to hurt a bit," he whispered.

"It's okay, the pain will be worth it."

He kissed my lips gently, then stepped back and removed his shirt. Once his skin was bare, I stepped forward and ran my hands from his chest down his abs. "So hot," I whispered.

Bending forward, he kissed the side of my neck, whispered, "With this bite, this mark, you become mine, my mate, my partner, and I become yours, forever after." His teeth sank into my neck and I sucked in a sharp breath, but the pain quickly morphed as a surge of power flowed from Caleb into me, the power heady and made me moan the next instant.

He licked the bite and whispered, "Make it quick, you three. The urge to mate with her is incredibly hard to resist right now."

Riddick stepped up behind me, swept my hair off my shoulder, and whispered, "With this bite, you become mine, my mate, my partner, and I become yours, forever." His bite hurt less than Caleb's, but the surge of power, though less pungent, spread through me. My head fell back and I let out a breathy moan.

Caleb stepped to the side, letting Triston move closer, he licked my shoulder and said, "with this bite, this mark, you become mine, my mate, my partner, and I become yours, forever." One more lick and then he bit my shoulder. I didn't even feel the pain this time, only the power surging into me.

My core was tight, and I was so wet it was dripping down the inside of my legs.

Branson stepped up next to Riddick, leaned down, and whispered, "with this bite, this mark, you become mine, my mate, my partner, and I become yours, forever." As he bit me, Caleb reached down and slipped his fingers beneath the thong and through my folds.

"Fuck, she's drenched," he whispered.

Branson pulled down my thong while the others stripped.

Once everyone was naked, I whined, "Please."

Caleb smiled and said, "Don't worry, my queen, we'll take care of you."

Triston dropped to his knees and began licking my legs from ankle up, cleaning up everything that had dripped down. He licked my clit, and I gasped, nearly coming just from that.

"On the cushion," Caleb ordered.

Branson laid me down on the cushion, my back on it, but my butt partially hanging off. Triston followed, burying his face into me, licking and sucking. I screamed and gripped his hair as I came, grinding against his face. He purred and it sent a jolt straight to my core. Standing, he moved to the side.

Caleb knelt between my legs and pressed against my entrance. "Are you ready, Ember?"

I nodded. "Yes."

He pushed into me, slowly, allowing my body to stretch and become accustomed to his girth. "Fuck," he said, drawing out the word as he slid fully inside. Dropping his head to meet my eyes, he said, "Sorry, sweetheart, but this isn't going to be a long session. The mating urge is so strong."

I nodded, not caring how long it was, only that he moved.

He gave me exactly what I wanted, thrusting hard and fast, I screamed his name as I came hard, and he snarled as he came and shouted my name. A thick, bright bond snapped into place between us, almost visible from the corner of my eye. Panting, he bent forward, kissed me, and withdrew.

I whined at the loss of him inside of me.

Caleb took a cloth and wiped his come from me.

Riddick grabbed me, pulled me to my feet, kissed me, then flipped me around, pushing inside of me. I put my hands down on the cushion to keep steady as he thrust into me fast and erratic. "Fuck, I get it now," he hissed.

Caleb chuckled, but I couldn't turn to look at him, my eyes full of stars as I came again, screaming Riddick's name. He came next and a second bond formed.

Triston laid me down, caressed my face, and pushed into me. "You are gorgeous, my goddess."

"Come for me, my tiger," I crooned, rocking my hips up to meet each of his thrusts. His bond formed and I nearly cried tears of joy.

Branson flipped me over as he lay down, setting me atop him and thrusting up in the same move.

"Yes!" I screamed, leaned forward, and dug my fingers into his thick chest. Adjusting my legs to allow me to ride him harder and faster, my eyes rolled up into my head as I came on him, my release drenching him. He didn't seem to mind as he roared his release.

High on endorphins and bliss, I nearly shattered when the fourth bond was fully formed, their magic flowing within me, and all four bonds glowing within my chest.

I started to fall, but Riddick caught me and carried me upstairs to a bathroom that was ninety percent shower with six shower heads and a rainfall shower head over the top. The tile was a forest green with silver and gold tiles randomly dispersed throughout it.

"This is beautiful," I praised.

He nuzzled my neck and said, "I'm glad you like it." Setting me on my feet, I kept a hold of his arm due to the lack of coordination I was experiencing. He kept an arm around my waist and smiled as he asked, "Legs not working, right?"

A surge of warmth, happiness or amusement, flowed into my chest. "Is-Is that your emotions I'm feeling?"

He nodded. "The bond will take some time to get used to and adjust. After a few days, it should settle fully into place."

Riddick walked in, ruffling his hair, and said, "It's a bit odd, but I like knowing how you're feeling."

"Can you guys feel each other?"

They both shook their heads.

"That would be extremely overpowering," Triston said, as he and Branson joined us. "Two of you in my head is enough."

"Two?" I asked, frowning.

"As their alpha and king, I can communicate telepathically with them and sense their emotions a bit," Caleb explained.

Riddick turned on all of the showerheads and I squealed as the rainfall one turned on, right over my head, drenching me in cold water.

They all laughed, and I realized he'd done it on purpose.

"You jerk," I muttered and rubbed my cold arms.

He wrapped his arms around me and said, "It'll warm up in just a second."

True to his word, it warmed up the next moment.

Stepping away, I asked, "Can I control the temperature on my own showerhead?"

He nodded and showed me how to work it. When I

turned it hotter, he and Caleb, who had been close by, stepped farther away.

"Are you trying to boil yourself?" Caleb asked.

I rolled my eyes. "Don't you know? Women take hotter showers to commune with our demons. It's the only way we stay sane." Stepping forward, I closed my eyes as the water poured over my head and face and down my body. Gloriously steaming hot perfection.

"So weird," Branson muttered. "I'd rather be in cold water than boiling water."

"Remember that quote and I'm sure our relationship will be great," I teased.

"I think Caleb will be the one constantly in hot water," Triston said with a snicker.

Caleb threw a loofa at Triston and it hit him in the back of the head. "Watch it."

Triston picked up the loofa and used it to lather himself up.

I should have been excited by all of the gloriously sexy naked men around me, but at the moment I only felt joyous contentment. Once I finished washing, I walked over to a wall where several towels hung and started drying off.

"Don't leave the bathroom!" Caleb yelled as he rinsed the conditioner from his hair.

My brows rose. "What? Why not?"

"We have another surprise for you," Triston answered as he shut off his showerhead and walked over to grab a towel. "We want to all be with you when you see it."

Sticking my lower lip out in a pout, I whined, "But I want to get dressed."

Triston pinched the tip of my nose. "No, you're a curious critter and want to go spoil the surprise."

"Fine," I sighed loudly and tied the towel around my chest.

Once they were all finished, everyone headed out of the bathroom, towels on, and Branson led the way to a door at the end of the hallway. He looked at Caleb, waited for a nod, then pushed the door open.

Branson and Triston walked inside while Caleb and Riddick walked behind me.

Stepping into the room cautiously, I peeked in, and gasped, immediately walking all the way inside.

This room was huge and in the center of it was a giant bed that had to be made from multiple king-sized mattresses put together, as I had never seen one that large anywhere before. The bed was covered in a thick comforter that looked incredibly soft and five pillows with matching pillowcases. There was a small fridge in one corner and a low table with a plush carpet and five cushions to sit on. The ceiling was all glass, allowing you to see the stars and moon easily. One wall had a sliding glass door and the other walls had pictures, dozens of pictures of us. Apparently, someone had been sneaking candid photos when I didn't notice. There was also a dresser with five drawers, each with our name burned into them.

"What is this?" I asked, spinning in a slow circle as I continued to take everything in.

"We're calling it our nest," Caleb said. "It's the place we can all go to be together. You know, for cuddle sessions or more sessions like tonight."

"It's ... it's so much more than I could have ever dreamed of." Tears slid down my cheeks as I fully accepted that I was no longer a hermit. No longer a lonely woman who had to resort to animals as companions. I was a mated woman with four amazing men who had created a place for us to be together, one where I would feel safe, comfy, and loved.

They circled around me, touching me in silence.

"Thank you."

"We told you, Ember, we will do anything for you and this is just the beginning," Riddick whispered.

"Do you want to see your bedroom?" Branson asked.

I nodded vigorously. "Yes, please!"

CHAPTER NINE

A week after our anniversary, our bond and emotions had settled enough to finally allow us to go out around others.

Our first stop was of course Caleb's parents' house. They fawned over us, inspecting everyone's bloodstones.

"Oh! I love what you did with yours," Jolie complimented me. "It's super cute."

"A diamond in the rough," Nico said with a wink.

Caleb rolled his eyes. "Don't flirt with my mate, Dad."

Pulling Jolie aside, I asked, "Did you get the crown?"

"Both!" she shouted.

Everyone looked towards us and she put her hands over her mouth and we huddled our heads together again.

"Yes, I got his and yours."

I sighed. "I don't want one."

She scoffed and rolled her eyes. "Darling, daughter-in-law, you are going to be queen whether you accept it or not. So, better to be decked out than to not be. You will crown

Caleb, a picture will be taken of you crowning him, and then he will crown you, and then we will take a picture of you and all of the current hybrids in your pack. Those pictures will be posted with the article about Caleb assuming the mantle of King of the Hybrids and list you as his queen. It will serve a dual purpose of announcing his title and your place as his mate. That way all those thirsty bitches will back off."

Laughing as I shook my head, I said, "Once again, you surprise me by the things coming out of your mouth."

"Are you all still keeping it a secret from him?" she asked, eyeing Caleb who was trying to stealthily move closer to us.

I nodded. "Everyone is in on it, so it's only him not in the know." And he hated it. He knew there was something we were hiding and he wanted to know so bad. I took a drink from the water Jolie had given me and winked at Caleb, which made him frown.

"How are you feeling?" Jolie asked. "Any pregnancy signs?"

I spit out the water all over Jolie as I coughed and gasped, "What?"

She wiped her face. "Well, that's the first time in a while that I've been spit on."

"I'm so sorry," I rasped and wiped at my face.

Laughing, she shook her head. "It's fine."

"Why ... why did you ask about that?"

"When you are mated, it makes you more fertile," she explained.

My mouth dropped. "No one told me that!"

She frowned. "Oh, well, yes."

"Is-Is there contraception that works?" It wasn't that I

never wanted to have kids, I just didn't want to have kids right now. Not with the H.E. trying to murder us!

"Let me call Kara," she said, pulled out her phone, and headed to a different room.

Caleb walked over, frowning. "What's wrong? Why are you panicking?"

My chest was pounding and my breaths were becoming larger and faster. "I, um, uh, fertile."

Riddick rushed over, grabbed me, pulled me into his lap on the couch, and started to purr. Immediately, my anxiety reduced. Resting my head on his shoulder, I pressed my nose against his nose and drew in big breaths of his scent to further relax.

"Mom, what did you say to her?" Caleb asked, growling softly.

"Do not growl at your mother," Deryn snapped.

"I'm fine," I called out to Caleb.

Riddick gripped me tighter. "What was it, Ember? What set you off?"

"I'm just not ready for that step yet," I whispered. "Maybe once the H.E. is gone, but not ... not now. It would be so selfish, so irresponsible. I can't do that to a poor, innocent child."

"You're not making any sense," Riddick whispered.

Jolie sat next to us, and said, "Okay, I talked to Kara and she has something for you. Do you want to go get it now?"

I nodded and pushed out of Riddick's arms, ignoring his growl. "Yes, please. Now."

"Need a teleport?" Nico asked.

"I haven't been to the elven lands or Kara's house yet, so yes, please," I requested with a nod.

"You haven't been to the elven lands?" Fox asked from down the hall, walking over to me.

I shook my head.

"Well, let's remedy that!" he exclaimed and set his hand on Nico's shoulder. "Trip for four, please."

Nico rolled his eyes.

"Five," Caleb snarled and stomped over.

"Oh, look at the time," Nico said, and teleported us.

I blinked as I inspected the cute house before us.

Kara walked out and frowned. "I don't remember inviting you, Fox."

Fox pouted. "Mom, you're so mean. Don't you miss your favorite son?"

"We all know I'm the favorite," Silverowl said as he and Leona walked out of the house. He smiled at me. "Congratulations, Rubyhare."

I dipped my head. "Thank you, Silverowl."

"Oh, she's already got the head dip instead of bowing down," Leona praised. "That's my little queen."

Sighing, I walked to Kara and hugged her. "Hello, I hear you have something for me?"

She patted my back and said, "Yes, let's go inside. Also, congratulations."

"Thank you," I replied and let her lead me inside of her home.

Katar sat on a couch watching television as we entered. He raised a hand. "Hello."

"Hello," I replied.

"Where're your mates?" he asked as we turned to head down the hallway.

"Probably breaking things at the house since we left them there."

Chuckling, he said, "They'll get over it."

"I'll just have to face a fight when we get back," Fox said behind us.

"Hello, son," Katar greeted.

"Hey, Pop."

"Why are we here?" Nico asked.

"I need to prevent pregnancy!" I shouted a bit too loud.

Jolie and Leona burst out laughing.

I sighed and shook my head. "Whatever."

Kara patted my hand. "It's perfectly normal, ignore them. They haven't matured past twelve."

"I'm sorry to barge in like this randomly," I apologized. "I wasn't informed about the fertility increasing after being mated. Now is not the right time for me, us, me."

She patted my hand again. "You don't need to explain yourself, child. I'm here for you whenever you need me. Especially now that you're mated to my favorite grandson." She leaned closer and whispered, "But don't tell him that. He's got a big enough head already."

Chuckling, I nodded my agreement. "Your secret is safe with me."

In a room lined with shelves that housed hundreds of bottles, Kara released me to walk over to a table where two white, plastic bottles sat. "You are going to take one of these pills every morning. It will keep you from getting pregnant and also decrease the pheromones you are putting out. That is part of the problem when you get mated, your pheromones go crazy and it sends your mate, or mates, into a frenzy to copulate with you."

"Got it," I said. "Thank you, Your Majesty."

"Nana or Kara, please." She smiled and slid the bottles towards me.

"That will take time to get used to, but I will try," I promised as I picked up the bottles.

"Come, while I would like you to stay longer, I think your mates are likely missing you."

Leona hugged me. "I'm so happy for you."

"Thank you. I appreciate your help in setting it up."

"So, how did it all go?"

I laughed and shook my head. "I almost teleported away."

"What?" Fox gasped. "We didn't hear about this.

I looked around at the living room of people and decided it didn't hurt to tell his family members. "I gave them the boxes with the bloodstones in it, gave a speech, and they just stared at it. Then Caleb started laughing."

"Laughing?" Jolie gasped.

I nodded. "I thought maybe I had misjudged everything and was about to run away, but he grabbed me and showed me my gift, bloodstones from all of them."

She blew out a huge breath of air. "Oh."

"So, we have bloodstones for sale, if anyone needs them," I said and laughed, shaking my head. Now, it was easy to laugh about it, but at the time, I had felt absolutely crushed.

"That had to be so traumatic in that moment," Leona said and put her arm around me, squeezing me. "Poor thing."

"Yeah, it was until he explained."

"Are you excited for the next steps?" Katar asked, turning his television off to face me.

I flinched. "Um, for Caleb becoming king, yes. For me ... not so much."

"You'll do great," he said nonchalantly. "The most important thing is to be there for Caleb. You are his partner, the one to help him shoulder his burdens. A sympathetic ear to listen to his complaints."

"Even when he's being a whiny baby about them," Kara said out the side of her mouth.

"Hey!" Katar gasped.

Everyone laughed, and I felt some tension ease.

"None of us set out to be princesses or queens," Kara informed me. "We just fell in love with men who were destined for that road and accepted the mantle. Just like you will. And, you at least have this support system of women who will be there for you no matter what you need."

"Thank you," I said, "sincerely, from the bottom of my heart. I don't know if I could have transitioned to this crazy life without all of you at my side."

"Girl bosses rule the world," Jolie said and held her fist out.

I bumped my fist against hers and Leona bumped hers against both of ours. Kara walked over and did the same, which earned a slight giggle and huge smile from Jolie.

"We need you all to keep us in line," Nico said and hugged Jolie. "Without our queens to speak reason, we would likely cause havoc and insanity."

"One hundred percent true," Katar said and winked at Kara, who blushed.

My heart soared seeing the older couple still able to make each other blush after so long being married. It gave me hope for my future.

"Well, let's get you home," Jolie said. "Caleb is likely fighting his other two fathers right now and who knows what your other mates are doing."

"Probably joining in," Fox said with a wide smile. "As we will when we get back. I do love an afternoon brawl!"

"Such a troublemaker," Kara said with a shake of her head.

"Bye! Love you!" he called out.

I turned and hugged Kara again. "Thank you, Your ... Kara."

She squeezed me and said, "Come see me again when you run out."

"Bye!" Katar called and raised a hand as he turned his television back on.

We teleported back to the house to find it empty.

"Grass sparring ring," Nico said with a nod. "I can hear the growling from here."

"I'm getting water to take my first pill," I informed them.

"We'll let them know," Fox said as he skipped out of the house.

Watching a short, buff prince skip out of a house was quite the sight and yet this was a normal part of my life now.

"Aside from this, are you doing okay?" Jolie asked.

I took my pill and nodded. "Things are going well."

"I'm glad to hear it," she said and reached into the back

of the cabinet next to us, pushing things aside until she got to the very back.

I watched curiously, waiting to see what she grabbed.

"Ah!" she exclaimed and pulled out a box of chocolate covered cookies. "I was saving these and I have to hide them so Fox doesn't find them, or he will eat them all."

I took one, crunched on it a bit, and around a full mouth said, "So delicious."

"Right?" she exclaimed. "So good."

"I need a stock of these at the house," I said as I looked at the cookie.

"I'll send Riddick the link and hint that you like them." She winked. "They like doing things that they think you don't know about and that make you happy."

"Good to know," I replied.

"So, tell me about it," she urged.

I blinked at her. She ... wanted me to tell her about sleeping with her son.

Seeing my expression, she laughed and said, "Tell me about the anniversary and the mating bonds."

"Oh," I breathed, finished my water to wash the cookie down, and launched into a full description for her, minus the sex parts.

She gasped when I mentioned Caleb laughing, but then smiled after I explained what happened next. "I'm so glad it all worked out, though not exactly like you had planned."

"Me, too," I said and sighed. "Though now I'm terrified about the fertility issue. It's not that I don't want kids, but ..."

She nodded. "I get it. And don't worry, the pills should sort it out."

"I wish I had been warned in advance," I said, "but we'll just move forward as we are." There were always things you couldn't control and didn't know about, and I would be damned if I let it affect my mood.

"Let's go grab the boxes so you can take them back with you," she said and shoved another cookie in her mouth. "You can't look at yours until Caleb puts it on you."

I drew an x over my heart. "Promise."

And I definitely would keep it. I really didn't want to look at the crown she had had designed for me. It might send me into a panic yet again.

CHAPTER TEN

Trusting, Branson, and I stood outside the gates of our pack lands, dressed nicely and waiting. Kieran, Ambrose, and Sheila were also with us, the first ones outside of our pack to join the clan.

Caleb and Riddick walked towards us, wearing nice shirts and slacks, and making my mouth water.

"Are you ready?" I asked with a wide smile.

Caleb shrugged. "Ready as I'll ever be." He stood before the symbol on the gate, and smoothed his shirt down. We had decided having the pictures in front of our symbol would be the best for posting.

Branson pulled out his phone, ready to take photos for our posts and to send to the media representatives that Jolie had set up.

Taking Caleb's crown out of the box, I walked up to him, smiling wide, and said, "As your mate, I am so proud and excited to crown you as our king. By placing this crown upon your head, I hereby crown you, King Caleb Fireclaw of the Hybrids." I had asked Fox for Caleb's full elven name to use for this event. It seemed appropriate as a hybrid to use our full names.

"I, Caleb Fireclaw, vow to do everything in my power to protect our people, provide a safe and welcoming clan, and rule fairly and justly."

Everyone clapped.

Riddick held out my new crown and Caleb turned to me, a huge, happy smile on his face. "As my mate, I hereby crown you, Queen Rubyhare Ember of the Hybrids."

"I, Rubyhare Ember, vow to rule at your side, provide you support, and do everything in my power to ensure the safety and happiness of our people." I'd spent so long agonizing over my response, but I still felt it wasn't satisfactory. However, it would have to do.

As soon as I said the words, I felt a jolt of power and then a warmth spread throughout my entire body. Immediately, I felt a new sense, one that pulled me towards our clan, and a sense of others farther away. I knew they were clapping, but I was too distracted by the new power to do more than blink.

"Can you feel them?" Caleb asked, seeing my wide eyes.

"This is how you sense other hybrids?" I asked, shocked.

He nodded. "Though, now that I've accepted the mantle, it is stronger."

"Whoa," I whispered. "It's ... intense."

"You're also able to sense those in our clan when they are in trouble," Caleb said. "It's something all royals are able to do."

“We’re going to head in,” Sheila said. She and Kieran had been spending a lot of time together lately and it seemed Ambrose had begun joining them as well.

“Thank you for joining us today,” I said. “It means a lot to us that you’ve joined our clan and support us.”

“Always, Your Majesty,” Kieran said and bowed. When he straightened, he gave a wink before the three headed through the gate and towards the house we’d built for him.

“Here, check the pictures I selected and let me know if they are good,” Branson said and held out his phone.

Caleb and I looked so happy and the crowns did look amazing. I had to hand it to Jolie, she had great taste.

“These are great,” I said with a nod.

“Okay, I’m sending to the journalists and to you all so we can all post to our socials,” he said and tapped away on his phone.

“Oh, I, uh, don’t have any social media,” I admitted sheepishly.

All four turned to me.

“Well, we need to rectify that right now,” Caleb said. He took my phone from Branson, downloaded a new app I hadn’t previously had installed, created an account, then pulled me against his side, held the phone up at an angle, and said, “Smile.” He took the selfie, then set it as my profile picture. “There, now your account is created.”

“Here, I’ll show you how to post,” Branson offered after sending the photos in our group chat.

After a quick tutorial on the app, I had a decent handle on how to use it, since it was relatively easy. However, they set up two other apps that were slightly different types of social media.

I felt like I could get lost for hours looking at the three different places with pictures and videos.

My phone pinged: "You've received a friend request from Princess Jolie."

"So, you do have to be careful who you accept friend requests from," Triston said as he looked over my shoulder. "Sometimes it's fake accounts, so it's best to check their mutual friends and confirm they are who they say they are. That is Jolie, though, so you can accept that one."

"Why would anyone create a fake duplicate account of someone else?" It seemed like a waste of time and pointless.

"Oftentimes it is for malicious reasons," Caleb answered. "Someone posing as me was messaging people asking for them to support a project and donate money. Once it was brought to my attention, I advised people about it, but there were several who had been scammed out of the money already."

"That's awful!" I gasped.

"Oh, and you are going to get people saying terrible things to you. Just delete the comments and block the people," Riddick said. "We can help if you want us to."

"I'll see how it goes," I said, finished my posts, and locked my phone.

With time to kill, I changed into workout clothes and headed into the backyard where we had a grassy area, much like Jolie's, for sparring and practice. Over the past month, I'd been spending as much time as I could improving my fighting and shifting skills. I'd also started learning more mage and elf spells and abilities. With us never knowing what was going to happen next, I wanted to be at my strongest and most powerful.

Three hours later, sweaty, and covered in grass, I headed inside to shower. Shockingly, none of the guys intruded. I was only a little disappointed. I redid my hair and put my crown back on, so it was one less thing to do later.

Jogging down the stairs, I found them in the living room playing a card game. "Are we ready to head to the celebration?" Dan, Emrys, and Katar had insisted on holding a celebration party for our crowning, one that was going to be a full red-carpet affair.

"Yes, we need to get to my parents' early so you can get changed," Caleb said.

"Right," I sighed. The dress I had on for the ceremony was pretty, but not red-carpet worthy. Jolie and Leona had purchased a dress that they weren't letting me see until I put it on today.

"Are we getting picked up?" Branson asked.

I shook my head. "No, I'm going to teleport us."

"Getting pretty good at it, huh?" Caleb asked. "I think I'm going to have to step up my mage training to get on par with you."

"I think it's good to have varied strengths in our pack," Triston commented. "Helps ensure in any situation we have someone who can handle it."

"Yeah, but what if we get separated again?" Caleb asked. "Whoever saves the others may not escape or get lucky enough to have Kieran show up."

Folding my arms across my chest, I narrowed my eyes

and asked, “Oh, are we fighting today? I thought today was a day for celebration and smiles.”

He exhaled and kissed my cheek. “I’m sorry. Let’s go. We can fight later.”

Snorting, I waved them towards me. “Let’s go.”

Once all of them had a hand on me, I teleported us to my bedroom in Jolie’s house.

“See you in a bit,” I said and headed out of the room.

My walk was stopped as Caleb grabbed my hand, spun me around, and kissed me so passionately, my legs were instantly weak.

He pulled back, kissed each of my cheeks, and said, “I told you that you were my queen. That crown looks good on you.”

“Such. A. Tease,” I hissed at him, grabbed his head, and pulled him down for another kiss before stomping out of the room and to Jolie’s.

She smiled when she saw me. “I knew that crown would look amazing on you.”

“Oh, your cheeks are flushed. Did you have pre-party celebrations?” Leona asked with a sassy smirk.

“No, but Caleb felt the need to tease me just after I arrived. That’s why I’m flushed.”

“Apple doesn’t fall far from the tree, obviously,” Jolie said with a shake of her head.

“Did you post everything on your socials?” Leona asked.

I nodded. “And we created accounts for me.”

“I added her as a friend already,” Jolie said.

Leona gasped. “And you didn’t send me a friend request, Ember? I’m hurt.”

"I don't really know how to," I admitted. "They gave me a one-minute crash course."

"Phone," Leona said, held out her hand, and opened and closed it as she waited for me to hand it over.

Obeying, I watched as she sent friend requests to herself, her mates, and Jolie's mates, too. She also added the kings and queens, but it didn't look like they posted much on theirs.

"I'm surprised the kings and queens have profiles," I said.

"They have people post for them most of the time," Jolie admitted. "On nights like tonight, they will post photos from the event, though."

"Well, now that we've sorted that, let's get changed and ready for tonight. It is going to be one hectic event for certain," Leona said with a shake of her head. "The kings are so excited to welcome Caleb into the fold that they spent a ton on this event and it's going to be extravagant, to say the least."

"Are there going to be a ton of people?" I asked.

They both nodded.

"Just stay with your mates, and you'll be fine," Leona said. "Or us."

"Okay," I agreed.

"Your hair and crown look good as they are, so let's just switch out your clothes and do your makeup," Leona said.

I saluted her. "Yes, ma'am!"

She smirked. "You know, now that you are queen, you outrank me."

My mouth dropped. "Uh, what? Oh." I guess I did. Leona was mated to Prince Silverowl, which made her Princess to the Elves, while I was now a queen. Funny how that worked.

"Well, Your Majesty, if you'll please step this way, I shall help you dress," Leona said with a curtsy.

Snorting in laughter, I once again found myself so grateful for these fun and wonderful women now being in my life.

I hoped our friendship continued for decades to come.

CHAPTER ELEVEN

Our normal SUVs were replaced with SUV stretch limousines. Leona and her mates would arrive first, then Jolie and her mates, and finally us. Since we were the ones to be celebrated, we were expected to arrive last.

"Just remember, you only need to tug on our bonds to alert us that you need a break and we will take you away from all of the people to a secluded room Dan set up," Riddick said as we neared the place the event was being held.

I nodded. "Right." The fact that Dan had thought to keep a room like that available for me made my heart soar. He truly was a kind and understanding king.

The guys had touched up their hair while I'd been getting ready with Jolie and Leona. The dress they had purchased for me was a bright ruby red, form fitted, and I wore a necklace of diamonds that was worth more than most people made in their entire lives. My crown was resecured with additional pins in my hair to ensure it didn't fall off. Caleb's magically stayed in place even when he canted his head. Male magic or something.

Hundreds of people stood outside the large event center we were heading into. Barricades had been set up to keep people back, guards lined the barricades and were interspersed in the crowd for additional security, and a long, red carpet went down the middle. The closest to the barricades were the reporters and journalists with their camera crews, ready to snap pictures of our first outing as rulers.

Caleb had been practicing his shield magic extensively with Nico and was able to now have a shield around us while we moved. Knowing that, I felt a bit easier about heading down the carpet with so many strangers around us and the H.E. still at large.

Finally, our turn. I took a deep breath and smiled at my four mates. "Let's do this."

Ezio opened the door and winked at me. "Good evening, Your Majesties."

Branson, Riddick, and Triston climbed out first, standing on either side of the carpet to wait for us.

Caleb blew me a kiss, stepped out of the limo, and raised his hand, waving and smiling to the crowd. After a moment, he turned back around, and held out his hand to help me out.

I accepted his hand, plastered a smile on my face, and carefully stepped out of the limo.

Cameras flashed in an almost blinding display, but I kept my smile on and raised my hand, waving as people called my name and cheered.

Caleb tucked my hand in the crook of his arm and we walked side by side down the carpet with Riddick, Branson, and Triston behind us. As we stepped between the barricades, Caleb's shield went up around us, invisible to those outside of it, and I found it muted the screams and sounds, allowing me to smile a bit more truthfully.

A dragon roared above us, starting to head down in a dive at us. Caleb's head snapped up, and he bared his teeth.

Before we could even move another step, Emrys stepped out of the building ahead of us, narrowed his eyes, and sent out a wave of power that had all dragons staggering a bit, even Triston. The dragon fell into the crowd and the guards within the crowd moved forward to capture him.

Caleb seemed immune to it, which had his eyes widening and eyebrows raising. With a renewed smile, we continued walking.

Emrys was back inside before most realized what had happened, so many didn't know if it had been Caleb or someone else.

The inside was colorful and full of sparkles and I realized matching my dress, which matched my eyes in rabbit form. The thought that they had matched those things had tears in my eyes, but I quickly blinked them away to avoid ruining my makeup.

"It's so sparkly and beautiful," I said as we passed through the foyer and stopped at the doors to the ballroom, where we would spend the rest of the evening.

"They put a lot of thought into this," Riddick agreed.

Two guards at the doors had us wait as we were announced inside.

"Now presenting King Caleb and Queen Ember of the Hybrids and their packmates Branson, Riddick, and Triston!"

The two guards opened the doors simultaneously, and we were met with applause and cheers.

Caleb's entire family was inside, including all of the cousins and uncles and aunts I had not met yet.

At the far end of the room was a raised platform with two thrones, empty and waiting for us to sit on them. Glancing around, I saw that each side had the same, with the kings and queens of the other clans seated already. Jolie winked at me from her seat beside Nico and I realized she had finally accepted her full mantle as queen now. She was no longer Princess Jolie, but Queen Jolie.

"Lots of changes tonight," Caleb commented. "It is definitely going to cause a stir among the population."

I nodded my agreement, as we walked up the two stairs to our thrones.

Caleb dropped his elbow, but laced our fingers together on the same hand, then raised his other hand. Everyone stopped clapping and cheering. "Thank you for joining us tonight. We are incredibly grateful to have all of your support and partnership as my queen and I step into our roles." Caleb sat first, and I sat next, following the protocol Jolie had explained to me.

"Long live King Caleb! Long live Queen Ember!" Thor shouted.

The entire crowd repeated the cheer, and I stared at the scene before me. Once again, the insanity of this life, the quickness from which I had gone from an outcast hermit to a queen was flashing before my eyes.

Dan walked down from his throne to ours, dipping his head just down enough to show respect without showing us as superior. "As is tradition when a new monarch is crowned, each of the fellow monarchs provide you with a gift."

What? Jolie hadn't mentioned this part.

Caleb's frown made me think he hadn't known about this either.

"While jewels have been a common gift, we understand the hybrid royalty while appreciating these items value others more. The werewolves hereby give you, King Caleb and Queen Ember, the Sapphire Island."

The crowd gasped, and Caleb's hand clenched a bit around mine as his eyes widened.

"Thank you, King Daniel. That is ... quite the gift and we will be sure to appreciate it for its many uses," Caleb said.

I had no idea what the island was or why it was important, but being gifted an island did seem a bit extravagant.

"We look forward to our continued partnership with the werewolves," I said with a smile.

Dan winked at me and went back to his throne.

Emrys and his mate came next. She was scowling, but it seemed that was a constant for Rhys's mother, who still hadn't warmed all the way up to Jolie. We had had very little interaction, so I wasn't certain how she felt about me. "The dragons have a long history of wealth and we hope the same for you as well. To assist, we are gifting you, King Caleb and Queen Ember, the mine of Morsai."

Once again, the crowd gasped and murmured while Caleb's eyes widened.

"Thank you, King Emrys and Queen Adelaide, we are humbled by your gift," I said, since Caleb was staring in shock at them.

"Yes, thank you, Your Majesties, for such a generous gift," Caleb said.

They dipped their heads before returning to their seats.

"You didn't know about this part either, did you?" I asked out of the corner of my mouth.

"Nope," he said. "And these gifts are more extravagant than any jewelry or item they could have given us. I think there's going to be a long discussion with my family tomorrow at brunch."

"I have to admit, I don't know what either of the items are," I whispered softer to ensure no one else overheard me.

"When I explain it later, you're going to faint in shock, so it's probably good that you do not know."

Kara and Katar approached, both smiling and full of warmth and sunshine. "The elves are excited for the new rulers' reign, and as such our gift is designed to assist with ensuring you can keep our people safe. That is why we are gifting you with fifty-fifty rights to the Carbac Mountainside."

Caleb sucked in a breath. "Thank you, King Katar and Queen Kara. That gift will be treasured for generations to come."

Again, something I didn't understand, but seemed important.

Nico and Jolie approached, smiling warmly. Nico said, "The mages are proud of the ascension of our son and his talented mate. We are excited to give you the gift of ownership of the mine of Perclane."

That one I had heard of. It was a crystal mine, the kind of crystals you could store magic in. owning one of the mines capable of producing those crystals would benefit us personally as well as allow us to sell the crystals. They were setting us up to be financially stable without their involvement. Clever, clever monarchs.

"Thank you, King Nico and Queen Jolie. We appreciate the continued support and partnership of the mages," Caleb said.

"Now that those formalities are out of the way, let the celebration commence!" Dan shouted.

A DJ started playing music and the crowd began dancing.

We stood from the thrones and walked down to hug Jolie and Nico.

"You all met and decided on the gifts, didn't you?" Caleb accused.

Jolie smiled wide. "Guilty."

"We wanted to ensure that no one could claim we were influencing or in any way responsible for your future success. We have given you tools, but it is up to you to take those tools and use them wisely," Nico said.

"I don't know how to thank you," Caleb said softly.

"That's what family does, son," Nico said and hugged him. "Now, take your queen out onto the dance floor."

Caleb took my hand and pulled me out onto the dance floor and as we spun around and danced with huge smiles, his other family members came to congratulate us.

The pure, joyful expressions on everyone's faces as we enjoyed the time together and a night of celebration were quickly ended as the ceiling exploded.

Caleb and Nico put a shield over everyone's head and the

debris slid down the sides of the shield, gathering along the walls.

"If the monarchs won't see reason, then it is time to end the monarchy!" a familiar male voice yelled.

Looking up, my eyes widened at my adopted parents and dozens of people floating where the ceiling had been, swords and other weapons in their hands.

"How dare you!" Dan roared and shifted into warrior form. "Wolves, attack!"

Every werewolf in the ballroom shifted and howled a battle cry.

"Mages, protect and attack!" Nico ordered.

A dozen mages materialized staffs and started glowing.

"Dragons, attack!" Emrys roared. "Kill them all!"

"Elves, attack and heal!" Katar yelled.

"Hybrids, kill them all!" Caleb roared, shifting into a meld of all of the races into a complex warrior form.

I shifted into my warrior form and my adopted parents' eyes widened.

"They're mine," I growled, the anger and fury of all those around me feeding into mine.

"Ours," Caleb corrected. "We stay together."

"Now!" my adopted mother screamed.

Chaos broke loose as they dropped down into the ballroom and flooded it, as we quickly learned there were far more waiting outside to come in as well. Hundreds streamed in, but my pack had eyes for two people alone.

My adopted parents tried to stay off to the side, four people as guards around them.

Branson, Riddick, and Triston made short work of the four guards, and my parents stared at us in surprise.

Mother started to reach into her pocket for something, but I jumped forward using my rabbit-human combined legs, and kicked her in her stomach, sending her flying into the wall behind her.

Dad spun to help her, but Caleb sprinted forward, grabbed him by the throat, and slammed him against the wall next to where Mom was slumped.

"You thought you could win with your overwhelming numbers, but since that trap where you almost defeated us, we've been doing nothing except prepare for you," Caleb snarled in his face.

"You will all die," Dad spat.

Some of their people tried to intervene, but Riddick, Branson, and Triston made an impenetrable wall.

"There's one thing you didn't count on, *Dad*," I said.

"And what was that, *child*?"

He had no idea the extra training, the super secretive training, that I had been doing with Jolie and Leona. The tricks they taught me that were only possible once I was mated. Once I was part of each clan, once I was queen. "We outrank every one of your members." Turning around, I faced the crowd, felt down the bonds I held with my four mates, to each of the four clans. Using a combination of my siren and mage magic, and the bonds that allowed me to access each of the clans, I sang as loudly as I could, "Enemies of mine shall bow before their queens!" It was a spell Jolie, Leona, and I had come up with. One that forced those of a lower rank when in the presence of one of their queens, to immediately bow. It was something we had prepared as we had assumed they might attack tonight while all of the kings and queens were gathered.

Every single enemy dropped to their knees, heads bowed and forced to still.

Mom gasped. "What ... how?"

"I told you, I outrank your people now." Turning, I gave her a smile and said, "And I'm not the weak child with abandonment issues you fought previously."

"Nicely done!" Jolie praised. "That's my girl!"

"That's my sirenling!" Leona cheered.

Walking closer to my adopted mother, I said, "You see, it took me finding them to understand what true motherly love is like. You are nothing more than a therapy topic now. Otherwise, you are nothing."

Her face contorted in rage and she tried to stab me with a knife I hadn't seen her pull out of her pocket. I kicked her again, but due to how close we were to the wall, she hit it much harder this time and her head made a sickening crunch before she slid to the ground. Dead.

"No!" Dad screamed and tried to attack me, but Caleb snapped his neck and took two large steps to stand between me and their bodies, blocking my view.

He hugged me and kissed the side of my head, avoiding my crown. "You did great, Ember."

I nodded. "Is it finally over?"

"For now," he said with a nod. "There may be stragglers, but we will find them and eradicate them as well."

Soft, warm hands pulled me away from Caleb and into a tight hug between two bodies. Jolie and Leona.

"You did great, Ember. We're so proud of you," Leona said as she stroked her hand down my hair.

Tears built in my eyes and fell down my cheeks, so I pressed my face against her chest. "They're dead."

Jolie patted my back. "Yes, they are. They can't hurt you anymore."

"It hurts," I whispered. "I know it needed to happen, I knew it was going to happen, but ... it hurts."

"Yes, death is almost always painful. Just know that it was them who forced your hand. They could have left you alone, they could have let you be, but they didn't and you did what had to be done," Leona whispered.

"Come on, let's go home," Riddick said behind me. He extricated me from their arms, put an arm around my shoulders, and gently turned my head so it was against his chest. I let him lead me blindly out of the room.

Before we walked outside, Triston pulled a napkin from his pocket and wiped my face, cleaning up my makeup before we were to exit and face the cameras there.

"Ready?" Caleb asked and held out his hand.

I set mine in it and nodded. "Yes."

We stepped out into flashing cameras and those livestreaming the video. Questions immediately barraged us.

Caleb raised his hand, and they silenced. "The terrorist organization Hybrid Eradication, or H.E., is no more. We have killed their leaders, and those who dared attack the monarchs. Let this be a lesson to all; we are a united set of monarchs and we will destroy any who try to harm ours."

Taking a step forward so I was at his side again, I cleared my voice and said, "This is an open call to all hybrids. You have a clan you can come to now. A clan who won't judge you for your genetics or whatever powers you have. Come to us and join our clan. Let word spread that the hybrids won't be second class citizens any longer. We are and will always be equals with our pureblooded allies."

"Thank you for your time and your support," Caleb said and dipped his head in a sign of respect. Pulling me forward, our pack walked back down the red carpet to the waiting limousine and drove home to shower and rest.

The H.E. was finally destroyed.

CHAPTER TWELVE

Four days after the coronation party, the buzzer at our gate woke us at eight in the morning.

Groaning, I pushed at Riddick, who lay beside me. "Make the noise stop." We had gone to bed sometime after midnight, so I was still tired.

"Yes, my queen," he mumbled and rolled out of bed.

Rolling onto my other side, I cuddled into Branson's back. He ran the hottest of our pack and I rubbed my face against his back to warm up, sighing happily.

Riddick tugged on our bond and I groaned. "Dang it." Sitting up, I hurried to the bathroom, then got dressed before meeting Caleb in the living room to go outside. "Any idea what's going on?" I asked.

Caleb shrugged. "Riddick just tugged on our bond, so I assume someone is at the gate that we need to go meet."

Sliding my arm around his lower back, I tucked myself into his side and said, "Well, let's go see who it is."

We headed outside, walking down to the gate where

Riddick stood, waiting for us. A strange feeling was in my chest, but I wasn't certain what it was.

"What's up?" Caleb asked Riddick.

Riddick tilted his head towards the other side of the gate where two dozen people stood.

My eyes widened as I felt the connection to all of them. Hybrids. Two dozen hybrids. Ranging from an elderly man down to an infant in the arms of one woman.

Caleb pulled open the gate and smiled wide. "Welcome! Please come in."

A black SUV pulled up as the last people walked by us, so Caleb and I waited to see who it was.

Riddick and Triston were dealing with the newcomers and Branson made his way towards Caleb and I, in case we needed backup.

When the passenger door opened and Dan stepped out, we all relaxed.

"Good morning, King Daniel," I greeted.

"Good morning, Queen Ember," he returned. "I apologize for dropping by unannounced, but I'd like to discuss a proposition with you."

"Please, come to our home," Caleb said. "We are honored you have stopped by."

Ezio popped up out of the driver's side and asked, "Am I welcome, too?"

"No, please stay out here," I said and waved my hand dismissively.

His mouth dropped, and I burst into laughter.

"Of course you're welcome, Ezio. You can drive the vehicle inside so it's not blocking our drive, please."

Dan put his arm around Caleb's shoulders and whispered to him as they walked up to the house.

"I'm going to start cooking breakfast," I told Caleb as I jogged past him and Dan.

I had a sneaking suspicion that Dan's arrival timed with the hybrids' arrivals was not coincidental.

"Do you want help?" Branson asked, as he followed me inside.

"Sure, can you grab the large metal bowl from the top shelf?"

While he got the bowl, I opened the fridge and took out the pack of five dozen eggs, a pound of bacon, and a gallon of milk.

He rinsed out the bowl, then set it on the island for me.

"Pancakes or waffles?" I asked as I began cracking the eggs into the bowl.

"Waffles would be my choice," he said, "but pancakes are easier to cook multiple of at once, and if you're making it for so many people, the pancakes seem like the easier option."

"We need to buy more waffle makers, so I have the option to make multiple at once," I said and grabbed the flour to start making the pancake batter. "Pancakes are good, too, though."

"What?" Caleb shouted from the dining room where he and Dan were talking.

"Uh oh, sounds like something important is happening," Branson commented.

"Why don't you go check it out and report back?" I suggested. "You can be my spy."

He chuckled. "I'm a bit large to be a spy."

"You're the muscle part of the spy group, not the one who climbs through the air ducts, obviously," I said with a smile.

He swatted my butt as he walked by. "I like the way you think."

It wasn't often I made food for a lot of people, so I really wanted to do it right. Losing myself to the tasks at hand, I was able to get the food ready without distraction or interruption. When I finished, I smiled proudly at all of the food. "Breakfast is ready!" I shouted.

"We know," Dan said from the other side of the island.

I jerked my head up, eyes wide. Dan, Caleb, and Branson all stood, smiling as they faced me.

"Sorry, I didn't realize you were all here."

"That became apparent when I asked you something and you ignored me," Caleb said.

"What were you all talking about?" I asked. "What proposal did you bring?" I looked between Dan and Caleb.

"You know we have a few houses built already, enough for most of the ones who came today, but we need more," Caleb said.

I nodded. They had moved forward with building several houses deeper in the forest on the chance that our announcement would bring hybrids to us. Clearly, it had been a good idea.

"I've offered to send my construction crew to help build more, but I have a favor," Dan said.

"What kind of favor?" I asked suspiciously.

"I'd like to borrow Branson for a job. It's going to take him away for two weeks," Dan explained.

Being without Branson for two weeks would be hard. Even though our bond wasn't brand new anymore and had settled, that was a long time for such newly mated people to be apart. My eyes narrowed. "What kind of job?"

"Yes, it's a dangerous one, but that's why I need him. He'll be going with Ezio and a few others after a rogue wolf who has been murdering humans."

My eyes darted to Ezio on the couch, reading something on his phone.

"I don't like this," I whispered. Looking at Branson, I asked, "Do you want to do it?"

He nodded. "I've done a few retrievals like this and I'd like to help out. It's something that makes me feel like I'm doing good."

I could understand that, but it didn't mean that I had to like it. "Well, how can I say no to that now? I still don't like it, but I won't stand in your way."

Branson walked around the island and kissed my cheek. "I know it'll be rough to be apart that long, but I'll call when I can and be home as soon as I can."

"Now that that's settled, let's eat!" Dan said.

"After we eat, I'll take the rest to the hybrids that arrived," Caleb said.

Branson made a plate, and I realized it was for me when he held it out. Taking it, I gave him a smile and headed to sit at the dining table and eat.

Dan sat across from me and asked, "What are your plans now that the H.E. has been taken down?"

"I'm not sure," I admitted. "Find a job?"

"You don't need a job now that we were gifted the

mines," Caleb said as he joined us. "You just need to find something that you want to do. Something you enjoy."

"What are you going to do?" I asked curiously. Now that we had land and a place for hybrids to join us, he didn't need to travel around rescuing them unless they were in such a bad place they couldn't escape.

"I'm going to focus on getting everything in order for the new businesses we own and getting our clan fully established," he answered. "Then, I was thinking we should take a vacation. You know, since we have an island now."

There was a lot to do to transfer a business over, especially one like the mines and the harvesting of the herbs in the elven lands.

What did I want to do? How could I help Caleb and begin fulfilling my role as a queen?

"I don't know what to do," I admitted. "I want to help you, but it's all a bit ... over my head right now. I don't know the first thing about being queen."

"Helping me is a good start," Caleb said. "I could use your help with the businesses. Maybe as you learn about them and what it entails, you'll find something you're passionate about."

"There is a lot that will need to be done to set up the clan and incorporate everything," Dan said with a nod. "You won't have a shortage of paperwork and decisions. Plus, with the new additions to your clan, you are going to start getting busy with their issues and resolving them."

"We should probably have a database with all of their basic information," I commented and tapped my finger against my lips. "So, we can keep track of them and reach out to next of kin if anything happens."

"I can send you a template of how mine is," Dan offered. "I'll remove my people's information, obviously, but I'll leave Ezio as an example."

"Hey, I didn't consent to that. I don't want them knowing my address," Ezio said around his food. He winked at me, signaling he wasn't being serious.

"I've been to your house over a dozen times," Caleb said. "Cat's out of the bag at this point."

"Wait, I don't want Ember to see my birthdate. Then she'll know how old I really am," he said and shook his head. "I'll never be able to face her when she learns I'm over thirty."

Laughing, I shook my head at him. "You're ridiculous."

"You're only just now realizing that?" Dan asked.

Ezio sighed. "My alpha is so mean to me. Caleb, can I join your clan instead? You'll be nicer, right?"

"Sorry, brother, but you're stuck with him," Caleb said.

"Ungrateful whelp," Dan growled at Ezio, who smiled wider.

Watching the over fifty-year-old men bickering like a father and son was endearing. I could see why people flocked to Dan. Every interaction with him had me loving him more.

Someone knocked on the door and Caleb called out, "Come in, Kieran."

"How did you know it was him?" I asked.

Caleb canted his head. "You could as well if you had paid more attention to your connection to him through the clan bond."

"Wait, clan bond? Does that mean you can add people to a bond that isn't our pack, mate, one?"

He nodded. "As king, I am able to add people to our clan. Papa Dan and Papa Emrys walked me through it with Kieran."

Kieran walked in and smiled at us. "Good morning. I just wanted to report that the newcomers who are opting to live here are in the available houses. The rest are waiting for you and all are very appreciative of the food provided."

"Thank you," Caleb said. "Have you eaten yet? Would you like to join us?"

"Thanks, but Sheila is making us breakfast right now," he said.

Smiling, I asked, "So, how are things with Sheila and Ambrose?"

His cheeks reddened, and he cleared his throat before answering, "They're going well, thank you for asking."

"We happen to be in possession of some unused bloodstones, should you need them, just so you know," Caleb said with a wink.

Kieran's entire face reddened. "It's far too soon for that."

"Just keep that in mind for the future then," Caleb said.

"You're the hawk shifter, right?" Dan asked.

Kieran nodded. "Yes, sir."

"Are you much of a fighter?"

"You've got an entire pack of werewolves, why are you trying to steal people from my clan?" I asked with a scowl.

"Your clan, I like the sound of that," Kieran said with a smile.

"Well, you are," I muttered, feeling embarrassed.

"Kieran," Caleb growled. "Don't flirt with your queen in front of your king."

"I'll make sure to do it when you're away next time," Kieran said with a wink at me. Clearly, he was in a mood to get Caleb back for embarrassing him earlier.

"I have a lot of people, but I'm always on the lookout for talent," Dan said, answering me. "There being hawk shifters isn't well known right now, so he would make a great spy."

"Did I jinx us by bringing up spies earlier?" I asked Branson.

He chuckled. "Seems that way."

"Well, the decision is ultimately up to Kieran," Caleb said. "I know you were looking for work, Kieran, and Dan pays well."

"I'm not the best fighter, but I have been known to spy a bit," Kieran said and turned his head away from me.

"I better go greet our new clan members," Caleb said. "Thank you for your offer, and I look forward to seeing the construction crews."

Dan nodded and raised his hand in goodbye,

Caleb kissed my cheek as he walked by, and I frowned at my plate on the table.

While I was glad that the hybrids were coming out of hiding and had a place to go, I was a bit worried. What it the people who joined weren't good people?

"You need some enforcers," Ezio commented.

"Huh?" I asked.

"Did you not realize you said that out loud?" Branson asked.

"Oh, I voiced my thought aloud?" Whoops.

"It's a concern all clan leaders have," Dan answered. "As Ezio said, you need some good enforcers to back Caleb up. He can handle the number of people you have right now, but as you expand, he'll need help."

"There's so much to think about," I said. "I'm glad we have you all to help us."

"Hello," Nico said suddenly.

Everyone spun to find him in the middle of the entryway.

"Teleporting into another king's territory is rude," Dan commented.

"My son gave me permission," Nico replied with a smug grin. Turning to me, he crooked his finger. "Come, I'm going to help you with your wards."

"Oh, okay," I said and stood. I started to grab my plate to take it to the kitchen, but Branson set his hand on my arm, stopping me.

"I'll handle the dishes."

I kissed his cheek and said, "Thanks, Branny Boy. You're the best."

Nico waited while I put my shoes on, then led me down the drive beyond the front gate, to the edge of our property line. "Mark the spot you want the ward to start with your magic, imagine a red magical stake in the ground."

Doing as he said, I used my magic to create a red stake that stuck up out of the ground.

"Good," he said. "Now, walk around the perimeter you want to create and continue making the stakes."

"How far apart should I make them?"

"I suggest one every twenty feet or so. It doesn't have to be exact and the spacing being uneven won't affect it."

"Does putting them closer make the ward stronger?"

He shook his head. "No, but I like that your thought process went down that line."

"So, I have to walk the full perimeter?" It was a really large perimeter.

"Yes, which is why I'm here so early." He smiled. "At least you'll have me for company. I did ours by myself. Very boring."

We started walking, and I tried to put the stakes as evenly as possible, just because I wanted them even.

"Befriend any animals lately?" Nico asked as he trailed after me, walking just inside the stakes, sipping on a cup of coffee.

"I haven't gone out onto the property yet," I admitted. "This is going to be my first time going around the perimeter."

"Are you going to know where your property lines are then?" he asked, and frowned.

I nodded. "Caleb put up markers so we would know where our property lines are." I pointed to one by the tree near us, a small silver disc with our symbol on it.

"Sometimes that son of mine does smart things after all," Nico teased with a chuckle.

"Don't worry, I won't tell him, or that giant ego of his will expand and kill us all with its crushing weight."

Nico laughed and shook his head.

"Do you think it's harder to become king for an established clan or a new clan?" I asked.

"Since I was the next for the throne, Dad had spent a lot of time showing me the ropes to prepare me to take over. So, it wasn't that difficult to step into the role. We've been training Caleb to be the potential next in line for all of our clans, not realizing he would ultimately become a king to his own clan. There is a lot of groundwork to be done to establish the clan, but I think he's well equipped and ready to take it on."

I thought so, too, but it was reassuring to hear him say that.

"As for you, I know this is a lot and you're stressing yourself out with worry that you won't be good enough, but you've got this. You just have to be your normal, charming self. Help those in need, like you had been doing at your cabin. Be kind and compassionate. And the most important thing is to support Caleb and be there for him."

"Thank you, Nico. That was actually really helpful."

"I have my moments."

We lapsed into silence as I focused on the task at hand. As I got the hang of it, he started telling me stories about Caleb as a child, as well as Riddick.

It was nice to hear about the rambunctious kids and teenagers they had been. To learn more about them. Even though we were mates now, there was still so much to learn about each other.

"Okay, perimeter is done," I said and exhaled, wiping the sweat from my forehead.

"Great job. Now, you're going to raise the dome."

My brows furrowed. "Raise the dome?"

"Yes, that's what you're going to envision. I'm going to help you as you do it, so I can help reinforce it and make it stronger."

"Okay," I said, drawing out the word.

"It'll be fine. You've got this."

Nodding, I took a deep breath, and refocused. Holding my hands out, palms up, I flexed my arms, accessing my magic, and began. As the dome began to rise, looking like a translucent red bubble, Nico held out his hand and the bubble thickened.

Halfway up, my arms started to shake, my heart beat faster, and my breath began ragged.

"You're doing great," Nico praised. "Just a bit more."

Caleb tugged on our bond and I sensed some worry from him. Unfortunately, I could not respond as I was focused on the dome.

"Slow, deep breaths as you push through," Nico instructed.

"What's going on?" Caleb asked, panting a bit as he clearly had just run here.

"Making ward," I panted and grit my teeth.

"Lend your mate some help," Nico said.

Caleb set his hand on my shoulder and I gasped as a surge of power from my core spread.

"What was that?"

"You can access your mates' powers," Nico explained. "That's why Jolie can shift."

So, I could shift into any of their forms?

Now wasn't the time to discuss, now was the time to finish the ward. With the additional power, it went much easier and it finished much faster.

Once it was done, I lowered my hands and took a gasping breath. "That sucked."

Caleb smoothed back my hair. “Want me to carry you back to the house?”

“No, I still have some questions for Nico, so the walk will give me time to explore our land and talk.”

“Okay, I’m going to go back to the new hybrids. I got worried because you were being drained of magic, feeling weak, and then you didn’t respond.”

“I was a little preoccupied, so I couldn’t respond,” I explained.

“If you’re good, you can just tap twice on the bond to let me know you’re okay.”

“We should come up with a standard system that we all use,” I suggested.

“My parents have one that works really well, so we can steal theirs,” Caleb offered.

“Sure, steal all of our good ideas,” Nico said and scoffed with his arms folded, but quickly smiled.

“I’ll write it up in our shared chat so you have it to review,” Caleb said, kissed the side of my head, and jogged away from us.

Nico and I began walking and he asked, “So, questions?”

“Can you tell me more about using their powers through the mate bond? I knew Jolie could growl and sense your emotions, but I assumed that was because of her being a siren. I know she can tap into you to be stronger and increase her stamina, but I didn’t know she could also shift.”

“Yes, you can tap into their strength, stamina, and all of their powers. With you being the first hybrid mates we’ve encountered, I’m not honestly one hundred percent certain what that will entail for you. I assume you should be able to shift into any of their forms, but we would have to experiment with that and find out. Jolie does it by focusing on the bond for who she wants to tap into and accesses their powers that way. She can also reach through to that clan, and affect those who are part of that clan. Again, I have no idea what you could do since you guys aren't connected to the clans you vary from. I am itching to have you test all of this out." He tapped his cheek. "What are your plans for the rest of the day?"

"Apparently it is to be a guinea pig for the Mage King," I teased.

He smiled wide. "Perfect! Can I invite the others?"

As we approached the houses where the new clan members were going to live, we found them all gathered in the center talking to Caleb. A few recognized Nico, their eyes widening in fear, and they bowed their heads.

Caleb noticed and said, "You do not need to be afraid of him. Especially not when he is visiting our lands." Caleb arched a brow at Nico.

Nico dipped his head. "I am a visitor and mean no harm, though I wouldn't mean harm outside either. Please excuse me as I pass through. I am borrowing your queen for a few hours, if that's alright with you?"

Caleb frowned. "What are you doing?"

I waited until I was in front of him and whispered, "Experimentation!"

He sighed and ran a hand down his face. "Why am I not surprised to hear you say something like that? Promise you'll be careful?"

I raised up on tip toe and pressed a chaste kiss to his lips. "Yes, my king."

He bared his teeth for a moment, but then changed it into a smile. "You may borrow my queen so long as you promise to keep her safe."

Nico bowed with a grand flourish. "I will keep my beloved daughter-in-law safe."

I turned to face the newcomers and smiled wide. "I'm very excited to have you all joining our clan. I shall meet with you tomorrow, after you've had a bit of time to grow accustomed to the new clan bonds."

We finished our walk to the house, and I was disheartened to find Branson had left with Dan and Ezio.

"Going somewhere?" Triston asked.

I nodded. "Would you like to come with me?"

"You don't trust me to go alone?" Nico gasped and pressed a hand to his chest. "I'm wounded, Ember. So wounded."

"I've got nothing else planned today, so sure," Triston agreed and slipped on his shoes. "Also, Branson said to tell you that he's sorry and he'll call you tonight."

I nodded and tried to squash the dejection I felt. I hadn't realized he was going to leave today or I would have said goodbye before I went to work on the wards.

"Do you need to grab anything?" Nico asked.

"Just my phone," I said and jogged up the stairs.

When I came back down, Nico set his hand on my shoulder and said, "Great! Time to experiment!"

"Wait, what?" Triston asked.

CHAPTER THIRTEEN

"Ember!" Fox yelled when we teleported onto the grass outside their house and his sword almost decapitated me.

Thankfully, Nico put a shield up, stopping it.

"Well, that's a rude way to greet your daughter-in-law," I said and scoffed. "And here I was starting to think you might be my favorite."

Fox pouted. "I'm sorry. It's Nico's fault! He knows better than to teleport here. He should have teleported to his lab."

"I was hoping to catch you all here," Nico said, looking at his friends. "We're going to do some experimentation."

"About that," Triston said. "What does that mean?"

"We're going to see what Ember is capable of doing through the mate bond," Nico explained.

"Oh! Yes!" Fox cheered.

"I've been curious," Rhys admitted from where he sat in a chair to the side.

"Where's Jolie?" Nico asked.

"Here!" she called as she walked out of the house, drying her hands on a dish towel. She hugged me and Triston.

"Okay, so first thing's first. Ember, tap into Triston's bond and see if you can shift into a tiger," Nico instructed.

Triston's eyes widened and mouth dropped. "That's possible?"

Jolie shifted into a wolf and back to human. "Yep."

"So cool," he whispered.

"Wait, does that mean they could shift into a rabbit?" I asked.

"For some reason, they aren't able to access my siren powers," Jolie said. "We think it's because my soul is the central repository for their bonds. I'm not sure about your form, though."

"Good thing we brought a secondary test subject," Nico said with a wide grin at Triston.

"I suddenly regret my decision to join," Triston whispered out the side of his mouth to me.

"Okay, me first," I said and took a deep breath, centering myself. Tapping into my mate bond with Triston, I pictured his tiger form and willed my body to take on that form.

"Well, that's interesting," Jolie whispered.

Opening my eyes, I frowned as I realized I was the same height, so definitely not in tiger form, but when I looked at my hands, I realized they were tiger paws. "Uh, I changed my hands only?" I asked and looked over my shoulder. My eyes widened at the sight of my fluffy, white rabbit tail.

"You took on your warrior form and added his tiger's paws," Nico said. "Fascinating. I wonder how many you could combine? Jolie can use all of ours at once, so you should be able to as well. Try to use Branson's bear form." He was practically vibrating with excitement like a child at a candy store.

"Should I call him to advise him? Does it startle you guys when she uses your powers?"

"I can tell you're using my powers," Triston said with a nod.

"Often times it happens and we do get worried and check in with her, so it's a good idea to let him know," Deryn said.

"I think they're just over protective and nosy," Jolie muttered. "Still, it wouldn't hurt to give him a heads up."

"I'll text him," Triston said. "Since your hands are ... well, not hands."

I flexed my hands and large claws slid out. "Whoa," I breathed. "These could do some serious shredding."

"Can you purr?" Jolie asked. "I bet you would sound super cute purring."

"She can purr," Triston said with a nod, his head down as he typed on his phone.

"What?" I asked.

"You've purred a few times, before with the connection we had, and at night when you're sleeping now."

"Is it adorable?" Jolie asked.

Triston smiled and nodded. "It is."

"Anyway," I said drawing the word out and distracting them.

"Okay, you're good to go," Triston said after his phone pinged with a message.

"Should I shift back to human or –"

"No, try it now. I'm curious what your body will automatically change on you." Nico cupped his chin as he watched me, clearly curious and excited.

I tried again, this time focusing on Branson's bond. As I drew on his powers, there was an odd *poof* sound and everyone gasped.

Opening my eyes, I looked down to see I was covered in brown bear fur. I still had Triston's tiger paws, which were his brown color, and when glancing over my shoulder, confirmed I still had my white rabbit tail. Reaching up, I felt atop my head for ears and felt my long, rabbit ears.

"Well, that's certainly ... interesting," Jolie commented.

"What form would she get from Caleb?" Triston asked.

"He can take both wolf and dragon forms," Nico answered. "Though, he prefers the wolf."

"As he should," Deryn boasted.

"He doesn't have an elf animal form?" I asked Fox.

Fox shook his head. "Nope."

"So, I should be able to shift into a wolf or dragon, too?" If I tried all of their powers at once, what would I shift into? "Okay, new experiment," I said and reverted back to my base human form.

"What are you going to do?" Rhys asked with a frown.

Closing my eyes, I imagined grabbing all four bonds at once and let my body shift.

"What the fu—" Deryn gasped, but grunted a second later.

Opening my eyes, I found I was taller than all of them, and could see much better. Colors were more vivid and I could hear sounds better.

Triston's mouth hung open as he stared at me, lifted his phone, and snapped a picture.

"Let me see," I said, then covered my mouth as my voice had deepened and there was an odd growl to it. Moving my hands back a bit, I saw they were once again tiger's paws and there was brown bear fur along my arms.

"You are slightly frightening," Jolie admitted as she walked closer to me.

"It's startling to see so many animals merged together," Rhys whispered as he circled around me.

Nico circled around me, snapping pictures as he went. "She picked great parts from each of them, though. The bear fur will keep her warm. The tiger claws will help her attack. The rabbit legs will allow her to jump high and kick hard. The cheetah or maybe tiger or I guess it could be wolf or dragon, too, since you all have similar teeth, anyway those will help her bite. The dragon scales along her neck and I'm assuming stomach will protect her from damage. The rabbit ears help her hear better. I'm not sure what the cheetah tail offers, but I think balance. Her eyes are still human, but glowing like an elf's does when they use their powers."

"I bet if she jumps too high, this time she'll use dragon wings to descend," Triston commented.

"Oh, that's a good point. She could switch and utilize other things while in a battle," Fox said with a nod.

"Come at me," Deryn said and waved his hand towards himself, beckoning me to come fight him.

Squatting down a bit, I engaged my rabbit legs, and dashed forward. His eyes widened as I cleared the distance quickly, my claws slashing towards his face. He dodged back and ducked my next attack. Shifting into his warrior form, he smiled as he fought me. As his fist swung towards me, I leaned back, finding that the tail helped me with keeping from falling as I leaned much farther back than I normally tried. Using my elf powers, I pulled roots from the ground and they shot up to wrap around Deryn's wrists, dragging him down to the ground.

"Behind you!" Triston called.

I jumped over Deryn's body, avoiding Fox's fists as he had attempted to punch me from behind.

Rhys and Fox both moved forward.

"This is just practice, right?" I asked, concerned since they had never ganged up on me before.

They both nodded. "We're just trying to gauge your abilities," Rhys answered.

Deryn broke the roots and brushed off his arms, a huge smile on his face. "I'm impressed already."

"Ready?" Fox asked.

I flexed my claws and growled, my tail swishing behind me. "Bring it."

The three darted forward, and I barely had time to register their moves, forced to react and act instinctively. Somehow, that seemed to work for the better, though.

Fox and Deryn jumped towards me from opposite sides.

Holding up my joined hands, I jerked them apart. Two large walls of rock thrust up out of the ground to my height, then sped in opposite directions, slamming into the princes and pushing them away.

Rhys shifted his head and blew out a huge breath of fire.

Crossing my fingers on both my hands, I created a magic shield that protected me from the fire.

"Nico! Why aren't you helping?" Fox yelled as he finally ran around the rock wall and tried to use vines to capture me, but with a downward thrust of my hand, they went back into the dirt.

"I'm observing," he said. "It's easier to do from here."

Caleb tugged on my bond, making me stagger a second. "Caleb's worried," I informed them as I continued to dodge attacks and try to cut them with my claws.

"I'll grab him," Nico said and disappeared.

"Break!" Fox yelled and dropped to a cross-legged sit on the grass.

Rhys and Deryn sat as well. Shrugging, I sat down, too.

Jolie and Triston passed out water bottles and we all chugged them.

Nico and Caleb appeared, Caleb scowling. He looked over at me and asked, "Are you injured?"

I shook my head. "Nope."

"She hit me with a stone wall!" Fox shouted. "Your mate is crazy."

Caleb smiled and relaxed. "Yes, she is. You good to go?"

Standing, I brushed off my pants and nodded. "Yes."

"Round two, fight!" Jolie called.

Rhys, Deryn, and Fox ran forward again, their attacks synchronized this time.

Smiling, I squatted down, waited until they were close, then leapt up and over the tops of their heads, landing behind them. Clapping my hands together, I formed a two-foot-thick dirt dome around them.

"Whoa," Jolie whispered.

Rhys burst out of the dome through the top in his warrior form.

I let the dome collapse as I ran forward and started attacking Rhys. When the others came behind me, I crossed the fingers on my left hand and put it behind my back. Deryn and Fox ran right into my shield, bouncing off of it with a grunt.

"What was that?" Nico and Caleb asked simultaneously.

With no time to answer, I spun around to take advantage of Deryn and Fox on their backs. I wrapped both in a bunch of vines and dragged them down into the grass, semi-burying them.

Rhys darted around my shield and swiped claws at me; they cut into my arm, making me yowl like a cheetah.

Caleb growled. "Dad!"

"Stay!" I ordered him, seeing him start to approach.

Fox used his powers to dig him and Deryn back out so they could rejoin the fight.

Taking a deep breath, I changed my throat, and exhaled a huge breath of fire. Deryn and Fox leapt out of the way and the fire continued towards Nico and Caleb.

Nico created a shield, eyes focused on me.

Rhys took advantage of my distraction, leapt forward, and wrapped an arm around my throat, claws at my jugular. "You lose."

"Dammit," I groaned, pouted, and reverted back to human form.

Jolie clapped. "That was really impressive, Ember. You've clearly been training in secret. Sneaky girl."

I nodded. “I wanted to be sure that I was ready should any new enemies show up.”

“Well, it definitely shows,” Rhys said.

That was high praise from the commonly quiet dragon prince.

“I’m impressed by how quickly you utilized their powers,” Jolie commented. “I wasn’t able to learn them in combination for a while.”

“I think it has to do with her being a hybrid herself,” Nico said. “They’re connected in a different way from the way we’re connected to our clans.”

“Does that mean hybrids are inherently stronger than purebloods?” Deryn asked.

“I think so,” Nico whispered.

Jolie scowled. “Well, that’s not something we want to be made public.”

“Why not?” Triston asked.

“Because then more people would view you as a threat,” Rhys answered.

CHAPTER FOURTEEN

Standing at a desk beside Caleb, my eyes hurt from going through the mountains of paperwork we had finally separated into piles.

It had taken us five hours to get through the basic items and next we were moving onto the more complicated tasks.

But first, lunch.

Triston and Branson brought us lunch, an indoor picnic of sorts, even in a cute basket.

Riddick stood from the couch where he had been working on a laptop on some other issue, and joined us on the large rug that was in the center of Caleb's office.

I ate some cheese, meat, and crackers, then sipped on the sparkling wine they'd brought. "Are we allowed to drink wine on lunch?"

"You'll have to ask the boss," Triston said.

We all turned to Caleb.

"As long as you aren't getting drunk, I don't mind a drink

or two at lunch. Plus, the queen gets special permissions." He winked at me.

"Good to know," I said and took another drink. The wine they had brought was incredibly good. Pulling out my phone, I took a picture of the label.

"Why did you take a picture of the bottle?" Riddick asked.

"Because it's really tasty and I want to make sure I remember which one it was."

Triston smiled. "Don't worry, my queen, I will add it to the list."

"List?" I asked, tilting my head slightly as I looked at each of them.

"A list of your favorite things," Branson explained. "Like those chocolates and the cookies with sprinkles."

My heart did a weird little flip in my chest at the knowledge they had a list of my favorite things that they shared with each other. I didn't say anything, but I also had a list for them as well. Though it was harder to find favorites for four of them.

"How are the new members settling in?" Caleb asked Riddick.

Riddick nodded, finished his food, and said, "Good. I spoke to Jolie and she's going to help us get a bus route to take the children to the nearest school. We also found some jobs for a few of them, but still have about six that are in need of one."

"We may be able to help with that as we're going through our new resources," I said. "We have a few jobs that need filled for the mines and the selling of the crystals in town."

"Oh, that's good to know. I'll talk to them a bit more about their capabilities and let you know." Riddick pulled out a small box from the basket he had brought and set a cute chocolate cupcake on my plate.

"Where's mine?" Caleb asked with a frown.

"Sorry, they only had one left at the shop," Riddick said and winked at me.

Caleb reached for it and I quickly popped it into my mouth. He growled.

I did a little happy dance in my seat as I ate the super sweet and delicious cupcake. *So good!*

"So, I was able to track down some of the remaining high-level members of the H.E.," Riddick said.

My head whipped around as I turned to look at him. "What?"

"We've been trying to track down the last remnants of the H.E.," Triston explained.

"I thought they had gone into hiding and we were safe for now."

Caleb said, "It is better to eliminate them fully instead of waiting around for them to try to attack us. I would sleep better at night knowing we have purged them from this world than to let them commit one more atrocity or put you at risk."

So, we weren't safe yet. That had my anxiety returning.

"Let's finish up our tasks here and head home to shower and change before our dinner plans," Caleb said as he stood.

"Dinner plans?" I asked.

He flinched. "Uh, yeah."

My brows furrowed. Why was he acting so strange?

Caleb opened a drawer and pulled out a black laptop. "Ember, can you review the workflow chart for the mine and also the five locations Riddick whittled down for the storefront?"

I stood, took the laptop and frowned at my name etched into the corner. "What's this?"

"Your laptop," Riddick answered. At my continued confused look he said, "We all have laptops, so it is easier for us to continue our work when we aren't in the office."

Our office was in the same building as the Council and Rhys's architectural office. They'd given us an entire floor, but we had only set up one office so far.

Sitting on the couch next to Riddick, I opened the laptop and frowned at the lock screen. "What's my password?"

"Caleb set it," Riddick replied.

We all turned to Caleb.

He smiled wide. "Your password is: rabbits rule all one word with capital r's and an exclamation point at the end."

Branson and Triston chuckled.

I narrowed my eyes at him. "I'll get you back for this."

He winked. "Anytime."

After logging in, I sighed at the desktop background. A picture of Caleb, shirtless, posing with his hands behind his head, flexing. There was a text strip over it that said, "Just for you."

Riddick looked over and chuckled. "Why am I not surprised?"

I refused to look at Caleb to give him the satisfaction.

Instead, I opened the documents he wanted me to review and covered up the picture of him.

First, I reviewed the five buildings that Riddick had found for us to use for a storefront for selling the crystals we were going to get from our mine. We wanted to sell some other things as well, but I wasn't sure what those things were. Triston was handling that part of things.

Two of the buildings were in outer areas, so the lease was cheaper, but it was also not as convenient or as heavily trafficked.

Three were in the downtown area, and one was much more expensive than the others even though it was a smaller square footage. While we didn't need a huge store, we also didn't want to get one that was small and wouldn't allow for expansion depending on what other items we started selling.

There were so many things to consider and it was not an easy decision. I made a list of pros and cons for my top two picks and saved it. "How do I send you my notes?" I asked. I knew the very basics of computers, having used them in school, but wasn't fully computer literate.

Riddick leaned over and explained how to use the email and showed me the list of saved email addresses so I wouldn't have to memorize them, and how to add attachments as well.

"Sent the storefront stuff," I said happily once I hit send.

"Thanks," Caleb said, his brows furrowed as he looked at something on his computer.

I opened the next item, the mine's workflow slideshow that detailed each of the steps and what staff were required as well as what each staff member was responsible for. I opened a spreadsheet, copying the information over so I could have a list of each position with their key duties, then highlighted the ones that were currently vacant, so we could talk to the clan members that needed jobs to see if they were able to do any of them. I also added a manager and two sales representatives for the storefront to the list since it was all part of it.

Truthfully, I wouldn't mind being one of the sales reps, but I knew that was out of the question as queen now.

"Why are you scowling?" Triston asked.

"Just thinking how being queen changes some things."

"Like what?" Branson asked.

"Like, I couldn't be one of the sales reps for our store, even though it does sound like it would be fun."

"Being a customer service person in any aspect is rarely fun," Branson said and shook his head.

Triston nodded his agreement. "Customers are often rude and expect to be treated with extreme politeness even when yelling at you. I've dealt with more than a fair share of assholes in my jobs."

"I couldn't imagine their faces if our queen was there, though," Branson said. "I doubt they'd be as rude when faced with her."

"Or they'd be extra rude because of the prejudice against hybrids," I countered.

"Trust me, love, you don't want to do a customer service job," Triston said and shook his head.

"You'll be too busy with other tasks anyways," Riddick said. "However, I don't think it would be a bad idea to have her there serving customers on the grand opening day. It would make for great pictures and articles."

"I'm willing to do that," I said with a nod.

"One perk you have over being king and an alpha is that people are less scared of you," Caleb commented. "If I were to try to work in the store, I would unintentionally scare people away just from my aura alone."

"Is that why you suppress it so much?" I asked. I hadn't really talked to him about it before, so I was very curious.

He nodded. "I spent a lot of time learning to rein it in. My alpha aura was strong even as a child, so the kids at the school were scared of me and gave me a wide berth even when I just wanted to play. Papa Dan taught me how to do it."

"Does it hurt or is it uncomfortable to suppress it?" It seemed like it would be tiring to suppress something that was just part of who you were.

He shrugged. "It's second nature at this point." Frowning, he said, "I'm doing it now, actually."

"What?" I asked.

Everyone turned to look at him.

He exhaled and I felt his aura press against my senses. My eyes widened as I realized how powerful he was.

"Whoa," Branson whispered. "You really do suppress it all the time."

"Except during sex," Triston commented.

I looked at him with a brow raised.

He smirked. "His guard drops while he's having sex and he stops suppressing it. I'm surprised you hadn't noticed."

"That's because she's too busy orgasming," Caleb said cockily.

Rolling my eyes, I returned to my laptop. "Riddick, I'm sending you the staff list with highlighted vacancies so you can discuss with the new clan members looking for jobs."

"Thanks," he said. "I'll talk to them tomorrow."

Caleb stretched his arms over his head and groaned. "Alright, let's call it a day and head home."

Closing my laptop, I nodded. "Sounds good to me. My eyes are burning from all the reading."

"Take your laptops with you," Caleb instructed and tossed Riddick and I black bags. One of the bags had a rabbit keychain on it, so I assumed that was mine and started to put my laptop inside of it.

"That's mine," Riddick said and held out the other one.

My eyes widened and he said, "I wanted something to remind me of you."

Chuckling, I took my laptop out and handed it to him. "You guys are so silly." I wasn't going to say how happy it made me out loud, though.

Triston and Branson packed up the picnic and we all headed to the elevator.

When the doors opened, we found Rhys and Fox inside.

"Hello," Fox greeted.

"Finished with your day of work?" Rhys asked.

Caleb nodded. "You guys, too?"

They both nodded.

"How are things going with your new positions?" Fox asked. "Any new hybrids show up?"

"We had a mother and daughter show up yesterday,"

Triston answered. "Daughter is about five and is a hawk shifter like Kieran, though a different kind of hawk. We introduced them and she immediately shifted and flew with him. Apparently, she's been dying to find another flying shifter that wasn't a dragon."

"It's so interesting the different animals you all can turn into," Rhys commented.

"I mean, elves shift into multiple types of animals," I pointed out. "So, it's not that unique."

"We don't usually shift into large animals like bears, though," Fox said.

"Which is also interesting to think about," I said. "Why do you shift into small-ish creatures only when we have shifters in multiple sizes?"

"I would love to do some lineage tracking on those with unique animal forms to see if it has to do with elven blood or not," Fox said.

"I'm definitely interested in that as well," Triston said with a nod. "It would be good to know more about ourselves, since so little is currently known."

We stepped out of the elevator to the underground parking garage, heading to our cars.

Nico teleported in front of us, grabbed Caleb and I by the arms, and said, "I'll teleport them to your house when we're done. You three go to your pack lands and wait there."

Triston, Branson, and Riddick nodded their understanding.

He teleported us out of the parking garage and into a sunny area, making me cover my eyes a moment before they adjusted.

"We received a report of a fight and I came to intervene, but I arrived too late," Nico said softly.

Opening my eyes, I gasped at the destruction surrounding us. We were in a suburban housing area and at least a dozen houses were destroyed, some still on fire.

"Did you catch the culprits?" Caleb asked.

Nico nodded, and we headed towards a small group of people, huddled in a loose semi-circle. The sound of a young child crying could be heard, but I couldn't see them.

"We did, but it wasn't in time to save one of yours."

"Ours?" Caleb asked.

"A hybrid was killed?" I asked, feeling anger brewing.

"Yes, but that's not the worst part," Nico whispered.

The people noticed us coming and broke apart, revealing a little girl hunched in on herself, crying so hard she was hiccupping, a blanket draped around her tiny shoulders. A smattering of blood over the side of her face that I could see.

Immediately, I ran forward, sliding on my knees on the blacktop, not caring about the way it tore into my jeans. "Sweetheart, are you injured?" I asked her, pushing back her hair so I could look at her face fully.

She looked up at me, tears streaming down her face, and after staring at me for a second, she threw her tiny arms around my neck. Her cries increased in volume as she clung to me. She was a hybrid; I could feel the pull to her.

Sliding my arms beneath her legs, I picked her up, and stood, turning to face Caleb. "Don't worry, little one, we've got you." She was injured, but her emotional needs seemed most important at the moment.

"I'm sorry," Nico whispered. "I wish I could have saved your father."

An orphan. The poor little thing couldn't be more than five-years-old.

"Do you have any aunts or uncles?" I asked softly.

She shook her head. "Papa was all. We had to hide. Hide because of what Papa and I am."

Tears sprang to my eyes. "No, not any longer, sweetheart. You're coming home with us. You're safe now and no one will harm you."

"Her mother was an elf and her father a mage and shifter hybrid, from what I could gather so far," Nico whispered to Caleb. "Her mother died shortly after childbirth."

"I'm taking her home. Can you teleport Caleb once you've finished talking? I need to treat her." I patted her back softly and rocked back and forth a bit on my heels to get her to feel safe and comfortable.

"Yes, go ahead," Nico said with a nod.

Caleb walked over, ran a hand down her hair, and whispered, "Don't worry, cub. We will take care of you."

She turned to look at him and asked, "Are you alpha?"

He nodded and smiled softly. "Yes, I am your alpha and king."

"Papa told me find you. I find you?"

He nodded again. "Yes, you found me, cub."

She looked up at me. "You alpha, too?"

I smiled. "Queen," I explained. "Alpha's mate."

Her eyes widened and she clung to me harder, putting her head against my shoulder. "I miss Papa."

Squeezing her tight, I said, "I know, sweetheart. I know.

I'm going to teleport us to our pack lands now, okay? It will feel a bit strange, but don't worry, you're safe."

She nodded against my shoulder and continued to cry and sniffle.

Teleporting to our house into the living room, I was glad to find Triston, Branson, and Riddick there. "I need my medical bag," I said urgently. "I also need someone to start a bath."

"I'll start the bath," Triston said.

"I'll grab the bag," Branson offered and jogged out of the house.

Her cries had lessened, but she continued to sniffle and whine.

Riddick looked at me with wide, questioning eyes, but I didn't want to discuss her parents' deaths in front of her, so I just shook my head. "Later."

"I'll go see if I can borrow a set of clothes from Theresa," he offered and hurried out of the house.

Branson returned and set the bag down on the cushion in the living room.

I walked down and sat on the couch, then set her on the cushion. She clung to me, not wanting to let go. "I need to look at your wounds, sweetheart. Can you please let go for just a bit?"

She sniffled and reluctantly let go. Tilting her head up, I smiled at her adorable little face. She had beautiful emerald green eyes and a cute little button nose. At her hairline was a deep gash that wasn't healing as fast as I liked. Grabbing the saline solution, I cleaned her wound, and checked for others, but it seemed to be the only one.

"What's your name?" I asked as I checked her eyes with the light, testing their dilation.

"Lily," she answered.

"How old are you?"

"Five." Her eyes darted towards Branson, who was hovering by the kitchen.

"Don't worry, he's one of my other mates," I told her.

"Bath is ready," Triston called from the second floor.

"Let's get you in the bath and clean you up," I said and scooped her up into my arms.

She set her head on my shoulder and her little fists gripped the sleeves of my shirt.

An intense protective feeling surged within me and I almost growled at the knowledge that someone had harmed her. If I could have, I would have tracked them down and destroyed them.

Triston squatted down and smiled. "Hello, little cub."

She ducked her head shyly.

"He's another of my mates, I have four, so don't be scared. They're all very nice and will protect you," I whispered to her as we walked into the bathroom. Triston had filled the tub halfway, which would help since she was small. There was also a fresh towel on the counter for her.

Shutting the door, I set her on the counter. "Okay, let's get these dirty clothes off and get you into the water."

She nodded and raised her arms straight up. Tugging her shirt off, I tossed it into the hamper we kept for our towels.

"Can you get your shorts off or do you need help?" I asked as I set her on the ground on her feet.

"I do it." She got her shorts off and walked to the tub, peering inside.

"Ready?" I asked, lifted her, and set her feet first, slowly into the water to give her time to acclimate.

She rotated and laid on her back, floating on the water, and closed her eyes. "I love water."

That was good to know.

Grabbing a loofa, I soaped it up. "Can you sit up so I can scrub you?"

She obeyed, but puffed her cheeks out. "I hate getting cleaned." Her eyes filled with tears and she sniffled. "Papa always did it."

Lifting one of her arms, I cleaned the grime from her and said, "I'm sorry for what has happened to you. It's not fair and not right. I know it hurts, but I will do whatever I can to help you and keep you safe."

She sniffled, wiped her hand across her nose, and asked, "I live with you? Here?"

We had a few guest bedrooms, so it wouldn't be a problem to give her one. Plus, I couldn't deny the desire to adopt her. I had already been contemplating it when I heard she was an orphan, but wanted to talk to Caleb first. Being asked by her now, I didn't hesitate to answer, knowing Caleb would be fine with whatever decision I made.

"Yes," I answered with a nod. "You'll live here now."

CHAPTER FIFTEEN

Once she was washed, bandaged, and clothed, we went down to the kitchen to get some food.

Caleb had returned while I was bathing her, and he smiled at her as he walked into the kitchen. “Hello, cub.”

Lily looked up from where she was perched on the counter, watching me pulling cheeses and salami out. “Alpha.”

He nodded. “Yes.”

“Her name is Lily,” I advised.

“Lily. That’s a pretty name,” he said. “Did you enjoy your bath?”

She nodded. “I love water!”

I set all the snacks I’d grabbed onto a tray, picked her up off the counter with one arm, and carried the tray in the other out to the living room. “Start eating and I’ll get you a drink, okay?”

She grabbed a cracker and nodded.

Crooking my finger at Caleb, I had him follow me into the

kitchen. He followed behind me silently. Once in the kitchen, I leaned close and whispered, "I want to adopt her."

He smiled and kissed my cheek. "I figured as much. We've already started looking for her birth certificate and other information. Unfortunately, her house was one of the ones destroyed, so she has no belongings."

Branson approached, a tablet in his hand, and slid it towards us.

I spun it so Caleb and I could see what was on it, my eyes widening when I saw an online shopping cart of girls' clothes and supplies.

"We knew as soon as we saw you with her," Branson answered my unasked question. "Caleb filled us in on the details. And we all agree wholeheartedly with your decision."

Tears filled my eyes and I sniffled as I wiped them away. "I don't deserve you four."

Caleb hugged me from behind and said, "Quite the opposite, Emmy. We don't deserve you."

Branson grabbed a cup from the cupboard and filled it with water, walking over to Lily to hand it to her. He leaned far over to hand it to her, like he didn't want to get too close.

She took it and quickly gulped it down, handing him the cup back.

"Mom said she knows of a trauma therapist some of the packs use, so we're going to make an appointment for Lily to go see them," Caleb whispered.

"You sure you're okay with this?" I asked.

He stepped to my side, turned me to face him, and said, "Yes. While I would love kids of our own, I have always envisioned myself adopting hybrids just like her, who need a family. I want to make certain she knows that although her parents are gone and we cannot replace them, we will be here for her for the rest of her life. And, I have a feeling we may end up with at least one or two more situations like this."

"Found family is some of the best family," Branson said as he returned to the kitchen to refill Lily's cup.

"I agree wholeheartedly," I said with a wide smile. "Is she really going to be okay with living with us? She's so young, will she understand?"

"She understands that I'm her alpha and staying with me is what she should do when she's separated from her parents," Caleb said with a nod.

I supposed that made sense. Pack animals sought each other out to gather together, even unconsciously.

"Order everything on your list," Caleb told Branson. "Also, find out her favorite color and order sheets and a pillowcase in that color."

"You want me to ask her what her favorite things are?" Branson asked, eyes wide.

"You're not the boogie man," I told him with a laugh. "You're large so lots of people are intimidated by that, but I don't think she is. For someone who needs protection, you might be her favorite if you let your guard down and stop distancing yourself."

He scowled, but took the tablet and went back to the living room to talk to her.

"I'm going to call Mom and let her know what's happening," Caleb said and ran a hand through his hair. "Knowing her, she's going to scream and get extremely excited as if it were our own child."

I smiled, knowing he was most likely right. Jolie was incredibly understanding and kind. I had no doubt that she would treat Lily the same as if we had our own blood related child.

"Oh, Branson should ask her favorite characters," Caleb suddenly said. "I bet she watches cartoons and we could find stuffed animals or items with those characters on them for her."

I nodded and headed towards the living room. "I'll do some recon, too."

Lily had finished her plate of food and was looking at Branson with a slightly canted head, as if confused.

"Hey, Lily," I greeted.

She turned and looked at me. "Hi."

"Was your food good? Are you still hungry?"

"Food yummy. Not hungry." She shook her head.

"What about ice cream?" Branson asked.

Her eyes sparkled, and she nodded. "Yes!"

Oh, boy. She already had the big man wrapped around her finger.

He left to the kitchen.

"Lily, do you have a favorite cartoon? Or favorite character?"

She perked up. "Alpha patrol!"

I frowned, not familiar with it. "Okay." I sent a text to the group chat so we could research later.

"Okay. Lily, can you shift forms? Are you a shifter?"

Her smile disappeared, her hands clenched the bottom of her shirt, and she looked at her lap. "Papa said no tell."

My throat tightened. After swallowing hard, I said, "I understand, but you can tell me. Remember, I'm the alpha's mate. Your queen, right?"

She pondered that a moment before she whispered, "Snake."

A snake? I hadn't even heard of elves turning into snakes before.

"Oh, okay. Do you know what type of snake?" If we could understand more about it, it would help us in raising her.

She shrugged and raised her eyes to look at me. "Lily show you?"

I nodded and smiled wide. "Yes, that would be great."

Crossing her legs, she closed her eyes, took a deep breath, and shifted into a beautiful albino python with white scales and red eyes. She was about three feet in size, roughly her human size.

My eyes widened and I felt a sense of fate, in my chest. She was me, but in snake form.

Branson reentered and froze when he saw her.

"It's Lily!" I shouted a bit too loudly.

Lily hissed and started to burrow in the couch.

"It's okay," I crooned softly. "I was just worried he wouldn't recognize you. You're safe, sweetheart. Please come back out."

She poked her head back out from between the cushions, her tongue darting out as she looked at us.

I held out my hands. "Come on, come into my lap, sweetheart."

"*Big.*"

Nodding, I said, "Yes, Branson is large, but it's his size that helps him be a better protector. He would never, ever, ever, *ever* in a million bazillion years hurt you."

Her tongue darted out again. "*Hear us now?*"

I nodded again. "Yes, I can hear creatures and shifters in their animal forms."

Slowly, she slithered out of the cushions, and curled up in my lap, resting her head atop one of my arms. "*Not scared?*"

I gently stroked her scales. "No, sweetheart, I am not scared of your snake form." Though, I could understand some would be. I also could understand why others might. It was going to be a pain for her growing up to have others judge her for the unique form.

She shifted back into her human form, still curled up in my lap, but now resting her head on my chest. "Safe?"

I nodded and stroked her hair. "You're safe with us."

"Ice cream," Branson said and set the bowl on the table. It had chocolate sauce, whipped cream, sprinkles, and a cherry on top.

I pouted. "Where's mine?"

"We have to eat dinner first, ma'am, before you get dessert," he chastised playfully in a soft tone. He was clearly trying his best not to startle her.

"Ember, you should get changed for dinner," Caleb said. "Dress with flats will work."

I looked at Lily, who was eating her ice cream. "What about her?"

"She's coming," he said with a wide smile. "I would never think of leaving her so soon."

"I'll be right back," I told Lily.

She nodded, her mouth full of ice cream, and whipped cream and chocolate sauce all over her face. How had she gotten so dirty so quickly?

"I'll stay with her," Branson said. "I don't need to change."

He was already wearing slacks and a nice shirt.

My eyes narrowed in suspicion at Caleb, but he just smiled and pushed me towards the stairs.

What were these men up to? Clearly, this wasn't a normal dinner.

As fast as I could, I changed into one of my simpler, but still nice-looking dresses, brushed out my hair and put it up into a ponytail, but pulled out a few chunks to frame my face, and did my makeup. Once ready, I made my way back to the living room.

All four of the men were gathered, watching Lily who watched an animated show on the tablet.

"When do we need to leave?" I asked.

"Now," Caleb said. "Lily, we're going to go out to dinner with some family. You're going to come, but you can bring the tablet to watch your show, okay?"

She nodded. "Be quiet at restaurant and let ..." her lip quivered and tears sprang to her eyes, "... Papa eat." Caleb picked her up, exhaled audibly, his breath blowing out over her face, and she visibly relaxed and rested her head on his shoulder.

"That's right, cub. You're very smart."

He had just used siren magic on her.

"Where are we going?" I asked.

"Can you teleport us to Mystics?" Caleb asked.

Mystics was a really nice restaurant that Leona had worked at for a while, until she was mated to Silverowl, and catered to royals and rich people in general.

"Mystics?" I asked with a scowl. "That's where we're going?"

He nodded. "Can you teleport to the sidewalk in front of it?"

Sighing, I nodded in return, set my hand on his shoulder, and smiled at Lily. "We're going to teleport again, the strange tunnel, remember?"

She frowned and put her arms around Caleb's neck.

Obviously, she wasn't a fan yet of teleportation.

Riddick and Triston ran into the room, putting a hand on me just as Branson did as well.

"Here we go," I said with a smile at Lily.

CHAPTER SIXTEEN

A few people gasped as we teleported near them in front of the restaurant, but thankfully, we hadn't teleported on top of someone. I had done that once and it had hurt to hit the ground right after.

"Ew," Lily whispered.

We all chuckled, understanding that gross feeling when someone else teleported you.

Triston pulled open the door for us, bowing and waving us in with a smile.

Caleb walked in first, whispering to Lily too quiet for me to hear.

I followed behind. In the back of the restaurant, off to the side, was a room where you could hold private parties and that was where Caleb headed.

Inside, I smiled as we were greeted with not only Caleb's parents, but Leona and her mates, as well as Dan and Ezio.

"Hello," I greeted.

Leona stood and hugged me. "Hello, sirenling. How are you?"

"I'm good," I said with a smile and walked to hug Jolie.

Jolie hugged me tight and said, "If it's okay with you, I'll come over tomorrow to help with Lily?"

I nodded. "I would appreciate it."

Dan gasped when he saw Lily. "Aren't you the cutest little cub ever?"

She tucked her head down against Caleb's shoulder and used her hair as a curtain to look at Dan through.

"That's my grandfather," Caleb whispered to her. "He's the wolf alpha. A very, very, very old wolf."

Dan frowned. "That's two too many very's, Grandson."

Lily looked over Caleb's shoulder at me and reached out. "Em."

Caleb frowned, but handed her over to me.

I put her on my hip, a leg on each side. "Let's go sit down," I said. "Do you want to sit next to me or in my lap?"

"Lap," she whispered, tucking her head down when Ezio looked at her.

Fox and Silverowl were zeroed in on her more so than the others.

"Yes," I said to them. "She's part elf."

"Do you know her form?" Silverowl asked.

"No," Caleb said at the same time I said, "Yes."

Caleb and everyone looked at me.

Sitting down, I positioned her in my lap, took the tablet from Branson, and set it on the table so she could watch her show.

"She's a snake," I informed them. Lily looked up at me. "A beautiful, white python with red eyes."

When I looked back at everyone, their eyes were incredibly wide.

"She's a rew, like you," Silverowl whispered. He looked at Fox. "That can't be random."

Fox shook his head. "No, it's definitely not."

"Water?" Lily whispered.

I started to reach for a water glass, but Jolie pulled a small, plastic child's cup from her purse, one with an animated character I didn't know, and set it on the table.

Lily took it and greedily sucked on the straw.

"Thanks," I said.

Jolie winked. "I kept a few things from Caleb's childhood in the hopes of having grandchildren in the future."

Silverowl and Fox whispered to each other, obviously discussing Lily.

"So, what called for this occasion?" I asked. "I was kept in the dark about this dinner until we arrived."

"First, we're going to eat and enjoy each other's company," Nico said. "After that, we can discuss the matters that brought us together."

Sighing, I pet Lily's head. "Fine. Be cryptic like always."

She giggled at something from the show, and I adored the cute sound.

"Are you hungry?" I asked Lily.

She nodded. "Nuggets?"

I glanced at Jolie, confused.

"I'm sure we can ask for some chicken nuggets," she said with a smile.

Lily looked at her and canted her head. "You ... different?"

Leona snickered and Jolie gave her a glare.

"Yes, a little," Jolie admitted, smiling softly at Lily. "I'm your alpha's mom. Your grandmother."

Lily thought about it a moment, her eyes widened, and she asked, "You give presents?"

Caleb coughed as he drank his water.

Jolie smiled, the obvious joy showing. "Yes, I will give you lots and lots and lots of presents."

Lily looked up at me. "I like her."

I smiled. "Yes, I like her, too."

Lily returned to her show.

I had thought the men who were my mates would be the last to steal my heart, but I had not anticipated this little girl. She had stolen it again. I wrapped my arms around her and squeezed.

She giggled and patted my arm. "No constricting! Not too hard."

Right, she was a snake that used constriction for its prey.

Loosening my grip, I said, "Right. No tight constriction. Only light, friendly constricting."

"Do you know what you want?" Triston asked me.

I shook my head. "Order for me?"

He nodded. "Of course, my queen."

Pulling out my phone, I searched the nearby area to see if there were any children's stores we could stop at after dinner. There was one about a block and a half away and it didn't close for three hours, so we should be able to make it.

I also started searching for the most popular kids' shows to read the descriptions.

"Your food, Your Majesty," a voice said, startling me since I had been engrossed in my research.

"Thank you," I said and put my phone down.

Caleb took a drink of his wine to try to hide his smile.

"Nuggets!" Lily gasped and waved her tablet at Branson. "Take."

Branson took her tablet, hit the button to lock it, and set it on the floor against his chair's leg.

She grabbed a nugget, bit it in half, and danced a little on my lap. It was incredibly adorable.

"Is it good?" I asked.

She nodded vigorously. "Yummy!"

"I'll add nuggets to our grocery order," Branson said and pulled out his phone.

I ate my food, a gnocchi dish that was divine.

When everyone had finished their dinners, ice cream was brought out for Lily and all eyes turned to me.

"The reason we gathered you here was to discuss something very important," Dan said.

"Oh?" I asked.

"We're going on a trip and we'd like you to come with us," Jolie said.

"A trip where?"

"The Summit," Nico answered.

"Um, isn't that the one where they tried to auction off Jolie?" I asked.

Leona laughed and Jolie scowled.

"They made her the prize for the tournament, yes," Dan said with a frown, but then smiled. "It didn't work out like Amos anticipated, though."

"Will it be okay to have all of us go? Won't that leave our new territory and clan unguarded and open to attacks?" The thought of leaving our new clan alone for a week terrified me.

Dan nodded. "That's part of why we're all gathered. Since we're all going and your clan will be the least protected, I wanted to offer you guards."

"The dragons and elves will offer guards as well," Rhys said, and Fox and Silverowl nodded their agreement.

Frowning, I looked at Caleb. "What do you think?"

"I think it's the perfect opportunity for you to see more of the world and for you to learn more about your role as queen," he answered.

Lily looked up at me with a frown. "You leave?"

"You're going with us," Caleb said immediately.

Her eyes brightened and she looked at him across the table. "We go trip!"

He nodded. "Yes."

"Who would be going?" I asked, looking at Dan and Jolie.

"Everyone here," Jolie answered. "Plus, the other kings and queens."

"Random question," I said. "Why do you all live in the same area when you could live in the different countries across the ocean?"

"It allows for us to have meetings together to come to agreements faster and to meet with the elders who are also located here. Hundreds of years ago, we used to be divided, a country per race, but that caused a lot of tension and there were lots of battles. We wanted to ensure our people could mingle and not be so closed-minded towards the others," Dan explained.

"Then why are hybrids so hated?" I asked. "If you wanted them to mingle, why are so many against the idea?"

"Long-held hatred is hard to get rid of," Rhys said. "We thought hybrids were a myth until the ones came to steal Caleb. We thought it was just physically impossible for dragons and elves to mate, like cats and dogs cannot crossbreed."

That did make sense, but was still so odd to me.

"How long would we be gone?"

"Two weeks," Rhys answered. "We will travel by train there and back and be there for one week."

"We will stay at the location to make it easier to attend the meetings and events," Jolie said. "We will have rooms next to each other as well."

"I don't like being gone for so long," I said, "but if that's what is expected and what you want, then I won't decline."

Caleb smiled. "It will be good for us to show up at the Summit, to make an appearance, and show our united front and lack of fear."

Lack of fear? That was a lie. I was terrified.

Nodding, I agreed to going, even though I did not agree with not being afraid.

"Great! We leave tomorrow!" Dan announced.

"What!" I screeched.

CHAPTER SEVENTEEN

After some of the fastest suitcase packing of our lives, and a shopping spree at two different kids' stores, we made it to the train station with five minutes to spare.

Lily had a few bouts of crying throughout the night, so we didn't get much sleep, which did not help with our attitudes.

She had shifted into her snake form, refusing to shift back, but thankfully allowed Branson to put her inside of his sweatshirt like a makeshift baby sling. She was coiled up inside while his arms were tucked up beneath her.

"You think she'll shift when she gets hungry?" I whispered to Caleb.

"I think she'll shift when she hears Papa Dan. He's got a super comforting alpha presence that children and women are drawn to. Used to make my dads so irritated when I would run to Papa Dan instead of them for comfort."

I could imagine the exact scowls the four of them would

wear, especially Deryn to have his father chosen by his son over him.

Dragging my suitcase as well as Lily's behind me, we boarded the train. Apparently, we had rented out the entire train for our trip since there were so many of us going.

"There you are!" Jolie exclaimed. "Cutting it close don't you ..." She stopped talking, her smile slipped to a frown, and she rushed over, cupping my face. "What's wrong? You've got bags under your eyes."

I glanced towards Branson and whispered, "Rough night."

She looked around and asked, "Where's she?"

Pointing at the bulge in Branson's sweater, I said, "Shifted."

Nodding, she said, "Once we start going, she should come out. It's not an easy thing to deal with when you're so young." She took Lily's suitcase and led the way through the train to the car that had our sleeping quarters so we could stow the suitcases.

Once that was done, we went to a car that had all glass walls and roof, allowing for the sun to come in and for you to see the sights as we traveled.

Leona looked up from her phone when we entered and smiled. "Hello. We were starting to worry you might not make it."

"Us, too," I said and chuckled as we hugged.

"Hello, Rubyhare," Kara greeted.

I made the rounds, hugging everyone before I sat on an open row that faced Dan and Ezio. "How come you're coming?" I asked Ezio.

"Perks of the job," he said. "I get to be bodyguard for His Majesty here as well as additional guard for you and the little cub."

"Where is my great granddaughter?" Dan boomed.

Lily's snake head popped out of the neck of Branson's sweater, right next to his face. Her little tongue flicked out, tasting the air, and looking around at everyone there.

"Hello, pretty girl," Dan crooned. He held his arms out. "Want to come sit with us and watch the scenery?"

She tried to slither out of the sweater, but Branson stopped her, lifted the bottom, and she slid out the much larger side there.

"Look at those shiny and beautiful scales," Kara crooned as Lily slithered across the train car towards Dan. "You truly are a beautiful elfling."

Lily stopped in front of Dan and after a pause, shifted into her human form. Dan patted the space between him and Ezio. "Don't worry, Ezio here is a friend. He's a protector that will help keep you safe. You understand?"

Lily nodded, glanced at Ezio, and climbed up onto the bench. Dan patted her head and she smiled up at him.

"I understand what your dads felt now," I whispered to Caleb, who finally joined us and sat beside me.

Caleb put his arm around my shoulders while chuckling.

"Are we ready to leave?" a man in a tuxedo asked as he entered the car, bowing his head.

"Yes, everyone is here now. Thank you," Kara answered.

He bowed and went back out of the car. Almost immediately, the train started moving.

Lily squeaked, but Dan patted her head and she relaxed as he pointed out the window. "Wave to the people, cub."

"People?" I asked, turning to see several cameras and reporters filming.

Caleb squeezed my shoulder, and we all raised our arms, smiling and waving at the cameras. "Don't worry so much, Emmy. I picked out the guards from each of the races myself to ensure the best would be protecting our clan. I also talked to all of our members and explained the situation. Kieran promised to work with the guards to ensure everyone's safety."

Exhaling harshly, I said, "I'm worrying too much, I know, but I can't help it."

Dan was whispering to Lily and when he laughed, she laughed, too. It must have been nice to have a grandfather like him growing up. Once again, I was jealous of Caleb and his upbringing. And now, not only were my birth parents dead, but my adoptive parents were dead as well, one at my hand.

"My queen, you're sad again. What thoughts are you lost in?" Caleb whispered into my ear, nuzzling his nose against my earlobe.

"Jealous of you and your support," I whispered, turned and rubbed the side of my face against his, chasing the tears away.

He made a humming sound in the back of his throat and kissed my cheek.

"Em! Em!" Lily called to get my attention. When I turned to her, she pointed out the window. "Fields!"

I looked out the window at the grassy fields, nodded, and smiled at the excited child. "Yes, grass fields."

"Those are best for mice," she said with a nod. "So many tasty mices."

"Mice, not mices," Caleb corrected her.

She puffed out her cheeks in annoyance. "Right. Mice."

Covering my mouth, I tried to hide my laughter at the adorable, annoyed face she made. Clearly, that was a word her parents had corrected her on repeatedly.

"Did you go to school yet?" Dan asked her.

She shook her head. "Too young, but ..." She paused, sniffled, and continued in a rough voice, "... was starting next year."

"We'll enroll you in the best school," Dan said and glanced at Ezio before looking at her again. "Do you want to go to a school of mixed kids or just one race?"

Lily pondered that a moment before looking at me. "Em?"

No matter what school she went to, she would deal with teasing and bullying due to being a hybrid and a snake.

"Maybe private tutors at first?" I suggested.

"Private toots?" she asked.

This time, I couldn't hide my laughter, and I ended up laughing so hard I clutched my stomach.

"Sorry, Lily, not toots. Tutors. A teacher who comes to your house to teach you," I said around my laughter as I wiped my tears.

"Oh!" she exclaimed, and then frowned. "So, no kids to play with?"

"You'll have kids from our clan to play with," Caleb informed her. Turning to me, he said, "Maybe we should see if we could set up a temporary school with tutors for the kids?"

Dan sighed. "We have a school already."

"Yes, but you know there will be teasing and bullying," I said quickly.

He narrowed his eyes at me and opened his mouth, but it was Ezio who replied.

"What if I escorted her each day?"

We all stared at Ezio.

"You want to escort her to school each day?"

He looked down at Lily, who was looking up at him. "Would you like to go to a school of wolf shifters? I would take you each day and if anyone is mean, you can tell me and I'll growl at them."

Her eyes lit up, and she nodded so fast I worried she might give herself whiplash. "Wolves are nice! And soft."

"Yes, our wolf fur is very soft," Caleb agreed with a nod. He looked at me. "Until we get more members and can establish a school of our own, it's not a bad idea. Ezio is one of the strongest wolves in the clan and I trust him with my life, so I would trust him with Lily's as well."

"Can I think about it more?" I asked softly, feeling that protective urge kicking in more intensely.

Caleb kissed my cheek again. "Of course. We don't need to rush the decision."

"Cows!" Lily exclaimed.

We all turned to see the cattle in a fenced-in pasture, eating grass. Why was it that people always pointed them out when driving or passing by? It was like it was a requirement!

"Rubyhare," Katar called, "come here, please."

Caleb squeezed me before dropping his arm. I kept a hand on the benches as I made my way to them, not wanting to fall. Silverowl and Fox sat across from their parents, and there wasn't an obvious open spot, so I hovered, standing, next to their benches that faced each other.

"You called?"

Kara tsked and Fox quickly scooted over, shoving Silverowl into the corner of the bench so there was room for me.

Trying to hide my smirk, I sat down beside Fox to face them.

"We were doing some digging and research after Silverowl reached out to us," Katar said softly. "We have found only one recorded instance of a snake shifter in elven history."

I perked up. "You did?"

"It is not a good account," Kara said and shook her head. "The previous rulers were terrified of the hybrids."

"Because we're stronger than purebloods?" I asked.

Both of them, as well as Fox and Silverowl, tensed.

After a moment, Kara ran a hand down her face, rubbing her eyes that had crow's feet now, betraying her age. "Yes. We don't feel that way, but it's terrifying to know there is a race that is stronger than you."

"You mean like the humans felt when they discovered werewolves, mages, dragons, and elves existed?" I asked with an arched brow and crossed my arms.

"Hey! Don't get sassy with us," Fox said and poked my side. "We are allies here."

Dropping my arms, I smiled. "Sorry, it's been ... rough for me lately."

"She doesn't have an elven name," Silverowl said. "We would like to give her one."

My eyes widened, and I glanced over my shoulder at Lily, talking animatedly with Ezio about something.

"An elven name?"

"Yes, we have all been talking, collaborating, to come up with a suitable name for her. Since you are adopting her, we want her to have all of the benefits of a child who would have been born to you," Kara answered.

"Everything is happening so quickly," I whispered. "It's terrifying and amazing at the same time."

Kara reached across and patted my hand. "I know, child. I know. We are here to support you in every aspect of your rule."

"Can you send me the list of names?" I requested.

They all nodded.

"We are each sending one," Silverowl said and smiled softly. "We couldn't come to a consensus, so we thought it best to leave up to you as her adopted parent."

"Does it still have to come from one of you as a pure-blooded elf?" I asked, feeling slightly irritated at that.

"Unfortunately, yes," Katar said. "We will work on some new legislature to change that, but in the meantime, you know we will assist you in whatever you need."

Smiling, I said, "I really do appreciate how accepting and

wonderful you all are. I'm so glad Caleb was able to grow up in a family as amazing as this."

Fox suddenly hugged me, squeezing tight. "I wish we could erase all of your negative past, Rubyhare. If we could, we would."

I patted his arm and let myself relax in his hold. "Thank you, Fox. That means a lot to me."

"We've heard rumors that snake shifters need extra warmth," Kara said. "You should look into winter clothing even in the warmer months for her."

Nodding, I said, "Thank you. That's good to know."

"I'll send you the snake research I did yesterday," Silverowl said, and typed on his phone. "They have some unique needs that other shifters likely don't share."

My eyes widened. Was I a bad adopted mother for not doing that myself?

"Thanks," I said softly.

Kara reached across and grabbed my hands. "Becoming a mother is terrifying, but becoming one so suddenly when you aren't prepared is a whole other level. We are here for you, Rubyhare."

CHAPTER

EIGHTEEN

After two days on the train, we were all excited to get onto solid ground and escape the "metal box," as Lily called it. There was a gorgeous estate with four mansions where all of the royals and guards, including us, were staying. Lily had immediately asked to play in the grass in her snake form. I'd shifted into my rabbit form and hopped and jumped around, making her hiss in laughter. After quick showers and a team of people to get us ready, we made it to the location of the Summit.

Lily asked me to carry her while we headed into the stone castle where the first day of the Summit was being held, a banquet. I wore a stylish red dress and Lily wore an adorable, fluffy dress that matched mine in color. Kara called in some favors from designers in the city nearby to get us the dresses in such a short amount of time. I did not want to know what the price tag for them was.

Caleb walked on my left, his stride confident and smooth, but I could feel his unease.

"Settle down, son," Dan whispered in his ear. "Everything is going to be fine."

Caleb exhaled and he nodded once, but his tension did not lessen.

"Sam!" Jolie screeched and raced forward to hug a man I didn't know.

"Jo!" he yelled with a huge smile as he hugged her tight. He pushed her to arm's length and said, "You look great!"

"You do, too. What has it been, ten years?" she asked. She tapped his crown and said, "It looks great on you."

"Your father is inside already, seated as the elder for the sirens," he replied.

Oh! He was the new King of the Sirens, Sam, her childhood friend. I remembered her telling me about him now.

"Sam, please meet Caleb's mate and queen, Ember. Ember, this is Sam," Jolie dragged him by the arm over to us.

I dipped my head. "It's an honor to meet you. Jolie's told me a lot about you."

He smiled and pushed his shoulder against Jolie's. "Don't believe half of it. She's a notorious embellisher."

She rolled her eyes. "Oh, please, you're the one who embellished every story, starting from us being three."

"No, that was Colton," he argued.

They both laughed, but his laughter stopped and turned into a huge smile when Leona walked up to join us.

"Leona!" he gasped and hugged her. "You look great. Being a princess definitely looks good on you."

"Being a king suits you," she replied. "I can rest easy knowing you're in charge."

He rubbed the back of his neck. "Stop it, you two."

"Sir, we need to head inside," a guard said.

"Right, see you guys inside," Sam said and waved before following the guard.

We waited until it was our turn to enter. The other kings and queens went first, then it would be us, and then the princes and princesses.

Two guards pushed open the doors to reveal an elegant ballroom full of sparkling people. All eyes turned to us as we entered.

"Smile and don't let them know you're scared," I whispered.

"Okay," Lily said.

"She was talking to herself, actually, cub, but it is good advice for you as well," Caleb said and chuckled softly.

The laughter eased the tension in all of us and we smiled freely as we walked down the middle of the room. To the right were five high-backed chairs where the elders sat. Someday, there would be a sixth seat, one for the hybrid elder.

At the head of the room was a raised dais where ten high-backed chairs sat.

I expected Kara and Katar or Dan to take the center seats, but my eyes widened when I realized they had left the center chairs for Caleb and I.

"Remember, you are going to stay with Branson while we do some quick alpha things?" I asked Lily.

She nodded and looked over my shoulder at him. "Bran Bran." She made grabby hands motions that might as well have been her clutching our hearts. So cute!

Stopping at the stairs to the dais, I turned and let

Branson take Lily out of my arms. Caleb took my hand and helped me up the stairs before taking his seat.

I took my seat, still smiling as I faced the room of strangers.

Most of the room was whispering to each other, clearly shocked to see us there.

An elderly man in a suit walked up to the dais, bowed, and when he raised his head, I swore I saw him narrow his eyes at Jolie before smiling. "Welcome, Your Majesties. I am excited that you were all able to join us. Tonight is the kick off to this year's Summit, which will feature two days of business and then everyone's favorite tradition, the tournament! And this year the winner will receive quite an amazing prize."

"I'm surprised they let Amos continue running this," Caleb whispered.

I was as well since I remembered the debacle of him putting Jolie as the prize the first year she had come.

"What's the prize, Amos?" someone shouted in the back.

He tsked. "You know the prize is announced the first day of the tournament."

"Good thing we're already mated," I whispered to Caleb, who chuckled and reached over to intertwine our hands.

"I'd destroy every male in the world to be your mate," he whispered and kissed the back of my hand.

My face heated and I squeezed his hand. "Sweet talker."

He winked at me, but returned to looking at Amos, who was frowning at us.

"Everyone, please enjoy your night of dancing and

mingling. Welcome to the Summit!" He raised his hands in the air and the music resumed.

People clapped and some swarmed around him.

"So, do we stay up here on display all night?" I asked.

"Are you hungry?"

I nodded. "Yes, but I didn't see any food?"

"They're about to –"

"Everyone, please head to the next room and take your seats for dinner," Amos announced.

"I see," I said, stifling my laugh at Caleb's explanation getting interrupted.

Lily raced through the people with Riddick right on her heels, scowling.

"Em!" she shouted and jumped up into my arms.

I caught her with a laugh and tapped the tip of her nose. "Hello, Lily."

"I told you not to run off like that," Riddick chastised her.

She frowned. "Rid mean."

Apparently, Riddick's name was harder for her to say, so she shortened it.

"No, he's trying to keep you safe," I explained. "Remember, it's important to stay with your guard, okay? All princesses have to stay with their guards."

She puffed out her cheeks as she nodded. "Okay."

"Come on, let's go eat," Caleb said.

"Nuggets?" she asked.

"I'm not sure," he replied. "We have to go sit down first."

She made grabby hands at Caleb and his eyes widened, but he immediately took her from my arms. "You're guard, too?" she asked.

He nodded. "Yes, I am one of your guards as well."

She smiled and kicked her legs on either side of him. "Yay."

He returned her smile and finally, relaxed. "Do you think we'll get dessert?" he asked her conspiratorially.

"Yes, please!" she shouted, getting a few looks from others.

Caleb laughed. "Well, we have to eat our meat first, remember?"

She nodded. "Meat then sweets!"

"That's right," he said and nodded.

"May I escort you?" Riddick asked and held out his bent elbow.

I slipped my hand through and smiled wide. "I would love that. Thank you."

"You look stunning in that dress," he commented as we walked. "And your crown definitely suits you."

"Thank you. I quite enjoy seeing you in a suit," I said and stroked a hand down his lapel.

His chest rumbled beneath my fingers as he purred. "Are you suggesting we should dress up more often?"

"I wouldn't be against it," I replied, which made him laugh.

Since there were six of us, we got an entire table to ourselves. Lily sat between Caleb and Branson, doing a little happy dance as she ate a buttered piece of bread. I sat between Caleb and Triston, though I was curious how they'd decided who would sit on either side of me. I'd asked once and they refused to tell me.

Triston buttered a piece and put it on my plate.

"Thank you," I said and had to refrain from shoving the entire thing into my mouth as I was suddenly starving.

Riddick reached across Triston, grabbed my water glass, and filled it.

Being taken care of by them made me smile and allowed me time to look around the room.

Most were talking amongst themselves, but there were a handful of people staring right at our table that had me on edge.

Caleb sat a hand atop my leg and patted. With the dress, he couldn't touch my skin, but the touch put me at ease anyway.

The food came and much to Lily's disappointment, it was not nuggets. It was delicious, and she ended up eating her entire plate without us needing to intervene. Her eyes lit up when she saw them bringing out large pieces of chocolate cake and as she put the first bite into her mouth, she did her happy food dance in her chair again.

I expected us to leave after food or mingle, but they asked everyone to return to the previous room where the daises had been removed, allowing for more room to dance. A small band was positioned in the corner, playing music.

Caleb spun around to face me, bowed, and held his hand out. "May I have this dance, milady?"

I set my hand in it and nodded.

We spun around the dancefloor, smiling and laughing as we teased each other. Jolie and Nico joined us and halfway through the song, Nico and Caleb did a strange synchronized spin that ended with Caleb dancing with Jolie and Nico dancing with me.

"Having fun?" Nico asked.

I nodded, letting him lead me around the room. "It's nice to not be worried about the H.E. and actually enjoy ourselves."

"Yes, but now you have a new issue," he said and then smiled. "Or should I say new blessing?"

Glancing in the direction he was looking; I saw Triston dancing with Lily.

"Yes," I agreed. "Blessing."

"Make sure you enjoy yourself thoroughly tonight as the next two days are going to be full of boring politics and arguments with the elders," he warned, kissed my cheek, and spun me into Caleb's arms.

"Hello, my queen," he purred and kissed me lightly on the lips.

We danced to two more songs before all agreeing it was time to retire for the night. Lily asked to sleep in bed with us and there was no way I could deny her when she looked scared.

I spooned my body around hers while Caleb spooned his body behind mine. "Don't worry, Lily. We will always protect you. You can rest safe with us."

She sniffled and said, "I miss Mama."

Petting her head, I nodded and said, "I know. I miss my mama, too." Or at least the one I'd had when I was her age.

Cuddling closer to me, she rested her head against my chest and her sniffling slowed until she fell into a deep sleep.

Caleb kissed the back of my head and said, "Go to sleep, girls. I will keep you safe."

"*We will keep you safe,*" Triston countered.

I nearly bolted upright, shocked to hear his voice, but didn't so I wouldn't disturb Lily. Instead, I slowly raised my head to find Triston, Branson, and Riddick on the floor around the bed in their animal forms.

Smiling, I rested my head back down and relaxed. Clearly, I wasn't the only one feeling protective of our newest pack member.

CHAPTER NINETEEN

The two days of business meetings at the Summit were more boring than I had anticipated. Mainly because there weren't any true disputes or arguments, just trade agreements, discussions of potential new business deals, and a few of the elders just glaring at Caleb and I.

Riddick was our guard for the two days while Triston and Branson stayed back to take care of Lily. Those three got to stay home and play together, something I was very jealous of.

As we exited the room on the second day, Jolie stretched her arms up over her head with a squeal and said, "Finally, sunshine!"

Emrys shook his head. "She speaks as though we'd locked her away for a month."

"Might as well have been," Jolie muttered. "The Summit meetings are somewhat useless now that we all actually communicate outside of it."

"True," Emrys acknowledged with a dip of his head. "These business meetings were really only necessary back when we were still at war with each other."

"Perhaps we can convince Amos, or whoever runs it next time, to have a single business day and the rest can be the tournament or we can just shorten how long the Summit is," Nico said.

"Let's head to the arena for the beginning of the tournament," Katar said. "I'm curious to see how many participants we will have this year since none of the royal family will be participating."

"Depends on what the prize is," Dan commented behind us.

"Well, thankfully Ember is mated or she might have ended up the prize this year," Nico said.

"Over my dead body," Jolie growled.

I patted her shoulder. "There, there. No need to growl."

The closer to the arena we walked, the louder the sound of the crowd grew. We stepped out of the tunnel and I had to close my eyes a second from the intense light difference from dark tunnel to bright sunshine.

Lily screeched and when I opened my eyes, I barely had time to get my arms out to catch her as she jumped at me.

Chuckling, I patted her back. "Miss me?"

She nodded. Looking over her shoulder, she gave Riddick a glare. "They made me learn."

Jolie laughed, but quickly slapped a hand over her mouth.

"Learn?" I asked.

"Maths," she said and hissed.

Dan stepped closer and patted her head. "Math is important, Lily."

She huffed and turned away. "No like."

I patted her back. "Well, no more math today, okay?"

She smiled wide as she looked up at me and nodded. "'Kay!"

Raising my head, my mouth dropped when I saw the stadium before us. The stands were full of thousands of people and we were headed to a terrace with a group of chairs that overlooked the oval-shaped sand arena and the stands. In front of the seats, the terrace was completely open all the way to the edge that dropped down sharply, allowing us an unobstructed view of everything. And for those in the stands to see us.

"Let's take our seats," Dan said and headed to his seat. When he stepped into the open, he raised his hand and waved and the stands erupted in cheers.

"Everyone loves Dan," Jolie said with a smile. "Even those not werewolves."

"He's always been very charismatic," Kara said with a nod.

Katar growled and she rolled her eyes at him.

"You two are in the middle again," Emrys informed us. "Lily can sit on one of your laps or in front of you."

"Sit with Em!" she shouted and put her arms up over her head.

He nodded and headed to his seats.

"We'll be standing behind you," Branson informed us. "So, just raise your voice or hand if you need us."

"Could you get me water?" I asked.

"Juice!" Lily exclaimed and raised a single hand.

Branson gave her a soft smile, put a fist over his chest, and bowed. "As my queens wish."

She giggled. "Princess, not queen, silly Bran Bran."

I tickled her side and laughed with her. "He is silly."

Our turn to walk out arrived and Caleb walked out first, raising his hand and smiling to the crowd. Many cheered for him, a lot of women squealed, and when I walked out, I had Lily raise her hand and wave. Her eyes widened when she saw all the people, but when they cheered and clapped for her, she jumped out of my arms and did a spin, making her pale pink day dress spin around her.

The cheering increased, and I was completely ignored. Outshone by a child. Had I not been as enamored with her as well I might have had my feelings hurt.

I sat between Caleb and Emrys, watching the little girl and knowing that although we could never replace her family, this found family seated together on the terrace would destroy the world to protect her and give her the best life possible.

She skipped over to me and put her arms up. I picked her up and set her on my lap sideways so she could see the arena. "It's fun here!"

I nodded and pet her hair. "Yes, you're definitely very popular. That's a good thing for a princess."

Once everyone was seated, Branson returned with my water and Lily's juice. He knelt on one knee as he held them out for us, making Lily giggle again.

Caleb rolled his eyes. "Show off."

Amos walked out, side eyeing us a bit, spun to face the crowd, walked out to the edge of the terrace. "Welcome to the Summit tournament!"

The stands erupted in cheers and claps. We clapped as well.

Raising his hand, he got them to quiet again. "This year, the prize is ..."

He paused so long that people started shouting for him to answer.

"... a trip to Atlantis!"

Everyone gasped, including Jolie. She turned to Sam who gave her a smile and an okay sign with his hand.

Sam stood and walked up to stand beside Amos. "I am excited to allow the winner and one person of their choice to join us in Atlantis for a three-day, two-night stay, with accommodations in the castle and all food and drinks provided. Atlantis can't receive many visitors due to our remote location, but we are beginning to open our borders and this is just the start."

The crowd cheered and whistled.

Jolie continued to scowl, but said nothing. Nico whispered in her ear and she relaxed slightly.

"That's quite the announcement," Caleb whispered. "They've never opened to outsiders before, well, outside of my dads going to compete for my mom."

"Wait, what? Why would they have to compete for your mom?" I hadn't heard that story before. Clearly, they had won, but what had happened to require it.

"I'll tell you later," he promised.

"All those who wish to compete, please head into the arena," Amos ordered.

At first no one moved, but all looked up at our terrace. After a few breaths, when none of us moved, dozens of men jumped into the arena. After several minutes, the arena was lined with at least eighty men.

"Why aren't there any women competing?" I asked Caleb softly.

He sighed. "The rules haven't changed yet to include women."

"That's ... archaic," I whispered.

Nodding, he said, "They're working on convincing them to change it, but Amos is ... stubborn."

"Em, I hungry," Lily whispered.

"Psst!" Jolie called, dragged a bag from the side of her chair, and shook it.

Lily hopped off my lap and ran over to her. Jolie set the bag in her hands, whispered in her ear, and then pushed her back towards me. Lily ran over and held out the bag. "Snacks! From Nana Jo!"

Nana Jo? I glanced at Jolie with an arched brow and she just smiled. Well, if that's what she wanted to be called, I was okay with that.

Taking the bag, I opened it and gasped. There were a ton of snacks inside! Crackers, cookies, applesauce cups, jerky, even some small sandwiches.

"How about a sandwich?" I asked Lily. If I gave her cookies first, she wouldn't want to eat the other foods.

She nodded and scrambled up onto my lap. When I tried to help, she hissed, so I stayed still and let her climb up on her own. Once she was seated, I took out one of the sandwiches, opened the bag, and held it out to her. I grabbed one for myself as well, then set the bag on the ground between my chair and Emrys'.

He glanced down at the bag and chuckled. "Jolie used to pack the same things for Caleb and Riddick when they were young."

"Children's snack preferences don't change over the generations very much," Adelaide, Emrys' wife, said with a shrug.

She rarely interacted with me, so I gave her a warm smile at her comment.

Lily looked around me at her and asked, "You queen, too?"

She smiled and nodded. "I'm Queen of the Dragons."

Lily looked back at Caleb. "She's your Nana?"

Caleb nodded. "Nana Addie."

Lily looked back at Adelaide. "So, Great Nana Addie?"

Adelaide's eyes widened a moment, but she quickly recovered and smiled. "Yes, darling. But you can just call me Nana Addie, too."

"She already knows she's great, so she doesn't need the reminder," Emrys said.

Adelaide growled and smacked his shoulder, but there was clearly no anger in the light smack.

"So many nanas and papas now," Lily whispered. For a moment she went still and I thought she might cry, but she looked up at me and asked, "Em can be ... Mama?"

Caleb, Emrys, Adelaide, and I all froze, none of us breathing.

"Lily needs a mama," she whispered and dropped her head, fidgeting with her dress. "Kids teased me for no mama."

How was this young child so observant and smart? Was she really as young as we thought or was the birth certificate wrong?

"Would you like me to be Mama and Caleb to be Papa?" I asked, feeling like I could barely breathe. I hadn't wanted to discuss this with her until much, much later. To give her time to grieve her father and accept that we were a good family for her to be raised with. I had not anticipated her being so smart.

She looked at Caleb and back at me, after a brief moment, she nodded vigorously while smiling wide. "Yes!"

And just like that, I was mush again.

Turning back towards the crowd, she gave me a reprieve to tilt my head back and hide the happy tears in my eyes.

Triston leaned over the top of my chair and wiped beneath my eyes with a soft napkin. "Best not to smudge that beautiful makeup."

"Thanks," I whispered.

He winked and disappeared from my view again.

Exhaling, I lowered my head and took a bite of my sandwich.

Lily swung her legs as she ate her food, humming a song I didn't recognize, and watching as those entering the tournament lined up to record their names.

Cameras from the stands flashed, taking pictures of us, the participants, and everything. I hoped they hadn't caught my tears, but honestly, that was the least of my worries.

Nico suddenly leapt up at the same time as Caleb, both of their hands up to create a barrier as a flaming metal ball stopped just inches from the men.

Spinning around, I covered Lily's body with my own, curling around her on the chair's seat.

The ball exploded and the stands erupted in screams of fear.

CHAPTER TWENTY

"Everyone alright?" Dan asked.

"Yes, none of us are hurt," Adelaide replied. "Good work, Caleb and Nico."

Caleb looked down at Lily's tear-filled eyes, spun around, and started glowing red. After looking closer, I realized that no, he wasn't actually glowing, I could just see his anger as an aura. "It came from there," Caleb said and pointed outside of the arena.

"I see them," Emrys growled and released wings from his back.

Caleb released his dragon's wings, turned to us and said, "Bran and Tris, stay here and protect the queen and princess. Riddick, with me." Riddick stepped up and the two took off, Riddick being carried by Caleb under the armpits.

I took my seat and put her on my lap again. "Whew! That was scary. Good thing Papa protected us."

She trembled a little, but I blew out a breath to spread some calmness, and she stopped shaking.

Jolie rushed over and sat in Caleb's vacant chair, smiling at Lily. "That's why people shouldn't play with fire!"

Lily laughed. "Fire, not for playing."

Adelaide sat in Emrys' seat, scales along her temples and neck. "Lily, do you want some water?"

Lily took the offered water bottle and drank from it, looking at the people in the stands who had returned to their seats once they realized there wasn't more danger.

Caleb roared from where he was fighting with whoever had sent the fiery ball at us and the sound echoed through my entire body.

Lily tensed a moment, shook her head, and exhaled loudly. "He mad."

"Yes, he is mad," I agreed, and pet her hair again. "He doesn't like that you could have been hurt."

An unfamiliar man teleported in front of us and within a breath, I had a shield around Jolie, Adelaide, Lily, and I. He hit the barrier with his fist and tried to use a spell against it.

Adelaide shifted into her dragon warrior form and growled loudly.

Jolie shifted into a combination warrior form, stepping in front of Lily and I.

Branson and Triston ran forward at the same time that Ezio and Dan did, the four of them apprehending the mage quickly, binding him with strange cuffs Ezio had brought.

It all happened within seconds, but felt like minutes to me.

"Good job," Adelaide praised me. "That was an incredibly quick barrier."

"It's almost automatic now," I said, chuckling shakily. There was ... something still wrong.

"You can let it down," Adelaide informed me.

I shook my head. "I can still feel ... malice. It's close."

Her brows furrowed and she started looking around. "Rhys!" she shouted and pointed into the stands.

I hadn't even seen the princes, but immediately, Rhys and Deryn jumped off the terrace. Rhys flew through the air while Deryn shifted into warrior wolf form and ran towards a man holding a strange object in his hands.

"Normally, I would blame Jolie for this incident," Adelaide said, her eyes fixed on her son fighting against the man. "However, I think this time I get to blame you."

"There's no blame to be given," Jolie said, her voice deeper as she used her mates' powers. "Just against those people attacking us."

"Are we safe?" Lily asked, clutching me as I held her in my arms.

I nodded, but didn't take my eyes off those around us. "Yes. Your nanas here are very strong and all the others around us will keep us safe. See, Bran is coming back with Tris to keep you safe."

"This is outrageous," Amos snapped as he stormed back towards us. He looked at me. "What is it about the women the princes choose? Why are you all so fraught with danger and –"

He didn't finish that sentence as Dan open hand slapped him across the face.

Everyone gasped, myself included.

Dan wiped his hand on his pants leg as though wiping

off filth. "You would do well to watch your tone and remember who you are speaking to. That is the Queen of Hybrids and Queen of Mages. They are my daughter and granddaughter. If I *ever* hear of you disrespecting them again, I will remove you from your place and you won't like our next interaction. I restricted myself with a slap so as not to alarm my new great granddaughter. Next time, I will let the women handle you."

Both Jolie and Adelaide had their fists clenched at their sides, looking ready to attack him.

Amos' face was dark red as he spun and walked away.

"Well, that had to feel good," Adelaide said. "Although, I'm a little upset that you did it before I could."

"I'll let you slap him next time," Dan promised with a wink.

"That man is mean," Lily whispered.

"Yes, he is a mean man," I agreed with a nod.

"Thanks, Dan," Jolie said and walked to hug him. "I don't think I could have held myself back if you hadn't stepped in. I don't care what he says about me, but bringing Ember into this was uncalled for. He's such an old, prejudiced bastard."

"Oh! Nana Jo said a bad word!" Lily yelled.

Jolie put her hand over her mouth. "Sorry!"

All of us laughed and the tension eased a bit more.

Caleb, Riddick, and Nico teleported to us, covered in soot and a bit of blood.

"Are you okay?" I asked as I rushed forward. "Are you injured?"

"We're fine," Nico said quickly. He looked at Dan. "What

were you guys doing over here? I felt Jolie's anger and then surprise."

"Amos overstepped and I corrected him," Dan said and brushed invisible dirt off his arm.

"Nana Jo said a bad word!" Lily announced.

Jolie groaned. "Of course, that's what she remembers."

My eyes returned to Rhys and Deryn fighting the man with the strange object and I gasped as they both fell to the ground on their backs.

Jolie screamed and jumped off of the terrace, dragon's wings popping out of her back as she dove towards them.

Nico teleported to them and started fighting against the man with the object.

"Fuck!" Dan shouted. "That's a magical bomb! Everyone, evacuate!"

The people in the stands had moved away from the fight, but were close enough I didn't doubt they were still in the blast radius.

I thrust Lily into Caleb's arms, shifted into warrior form, and used my enhanced rabbit-human legs to leap from the terrace towards them.

The man used a spell that knocked Nico out next to Rhys, Deryn, and Jolie.

Putting a shield around myself once near him, I said, "Not today, you bastard."

"You cannot stop me," he snarled. The sphere started glowing orange and I knew I had limited time.

Where could I send him? Oh!

I had to stop using a shield, but I just needed a single moment, so it had to be enough. Opening a portal beneath his feet, I sent him to my former home, to a section of the woods that I knew even if someone had moved in that they likely wouldn't venture to as it was surrounded by thick brambles full of thorns and was miles from the house.

"No!" he screamed and tried to jump up at the portal, but I closed it before he could.

My victorious smile was short-lived as a man with a knife leapt at me.

Lily screamed from the Terrace at the same time Caleb roared and people in the stands around us screamed.

Triston stepped in front of me, taking the blade to his upper right chest. The blade meant for me.

Riddick swiped his claws across the man's throat, killing him.

Triston stumbled back and I barely caught him before he fell. Gently, I lowered him to his back. "It's okay," I whispered. "I've got you. It's okay."

Triston smiled up at me. "You were brilliant, Em. It was smart to teleport him somewhere the bomb wouldn't hurt anyone."

"Stop talking," I snapped as I put my hands on either side of the knife and started to heal him. "Riddick! I need you!"

Riddick dropped to his knees on the other side of Triston. "What do you need?"

"You're going to have to pull out the knife on my command. You!" I shouted at a male nearby who I could sense was an alpha.

His eyes widened, but he quickly came over. "Y-Yes, Your Majesty?"

"I need you to help hold him down. He's going to react

when the knife is pulled out, but I need him to stay down," I instructed.

He nodded, then looked over his shoulder and said, "Tysen. Abraham. Come help."

Two additional men, both alphas, came over and they knelt around Triston, hands on him to hold him down.

"Ready?" I asked.

Triston closed his eyes and his heart began to pump slower. Shit! Was it poisoned?

"Kara! Poison!" I screamed, my heart hammering in my chest. Shit. Shit. "Okay. On three, pull the knife and you three hold him down. One. Two. Three!"

Riddick jerked the knife out of Triston, who roared and tried to get up, but the three held him down.

Closing my eyes, I focused on the wound and closing it.

"I'm here," Kara said and I felt her hands rest atop mine. "I'll extract the poison while you heal. Fox! Help heal!"

Fox set his hands on the other sides of the wound from mine. "It's okay, Rubyhare, we're here. He's going to be fine."

Tears leaked down my face and I couldn't speak, too focused on saving my mate.

"He's going to react when I start extracting, so hold him down harder," Kara ordered the men helping us.

"Yes, Your Majesty," they said immediately.

A hand rested on my shoulder and I sensed Caleb and felt our connection open more as he gave me some of his power. "Deep, slow breaths, Emmy," he whispered.

The stands were deathly silent as we worked, everyone waiting to see what was going to happen.

Kara started drawing out the poison and Triston roared,

howled, and hissed in pain, thrashing beneath our hands as he tried to escape.

"I'm sorry. I'm sorry. I'm so sorry," I whispered as I continued to heal him. My healing powers weren't strong enough to close the wound quickly, but with Fox's help, we finally got it closed.

Opening my eyes, I looked down at the peacefully sleeping Triston and nearly collapsed in relief.

Caleb knelt down and hugged me one armed. I wondered why he was only hugging me with one arm until I felt Lily's hands and head rest on my shoulder.

"He okay?" she asked softly and her hands trembled slightly on my shoulder.

"Yes, he's okay," Kara said and smiled at me. "Great job, Ember. You've really improved this past year."

"I couldn't have done it without you all," I said and looked at everyone. Then, I bowed my head. "Thank you for helping me save my mate."

"She's bowing to lower ranks?" someone asked.

"You don't have to thank us," the man I'd first called over said. "You saved all of us from the bomb. It's all of us who should be thanking you."

Caleb helped me to my feet and I stared in disbelief as the entire stadium dropped to their knees and bowed to me.

"Thank you for saving us, Queen Ember!" they shouted in unison.

CHAPTER TWENTY-ONE

After intense interrogation, it was determined that the people behind the attack had been former members of the H.E., and this had been their last-ditch effort to kill as many of us and our supporters as they could.

Nico had teleported to my previous home with Dan to capture the man, but they had confirmed the bomb had been one he couldn't release, so he had died when the bomb went off. The place I'd teleported him to had a new crater, but no one else had been injured as it was a secluded part of my lands.

Triston had woken up a few hours after the healing, starving, but otherwise fully healed.

Video of the event had spread like wildfire across the news outlets and social media. I was being hailed as a humble hero as images of me bowing to those who helped combined with an image of the people in the stands bowing to me were shared. The hybrids were finally being recognized as a positive instead of a negative.

After resting for a day, we got to go explore the nearby town and see the sights. Lily was just as excited as I was, and poor Ezio had to run all over to show her things he wanted to see. He kept her on his shoulders as he ran up to things she was too short to see on her own. The joyous smile on his face as she squealed or giggled in delight had me smiling even wider.

I bought a few souvenirs for myself and also ordered a chocolate sampler box to be sent to our house so we could share it with the clan when we returned.

Taking a deep breath, I exhaled loudly. "It smells so clean here."

"It's thanks to the ocean nearby," Riddick answered.

"I wouldn't mind an ocean property," I commented.

"We own one," Caleb said.

Looking over my shoulder at him as I stopped at a cute little bookshop, I asked, "What?"

"We own an island, remember?" he said with a chuckle.

"Oh, right! I forgot about that island."

"It needs a house built on it as it's currently just wildlife and wilderness," he explained. "There are a lot of natural resources and animals there that you can't find elsewhere."

"Wait, animals you can't find elsewhere?" I asked and looked up at him. "Are you thinking there are hybrids there?"

He nodded. "That's part of why Papa Dan gave it to us."

My mouth dropped. "Why haven't we gone there yet?"

"We've been a little busy," Triston reminded me and squeezed our joined hands.

Since his attack the day of the tournament, I'd been a little clingier than usual, but no one commented or seemed to mind. They likely understood my need to reassure myself that he was alive and well.

"We'll plan a trip soon," Caleb promised.

Perusing the books on the shelf, I grabbed a few children's books for Lily and a couple ones that looked interesting to me.

"You definitely don't need that one," Caleb commented when I picked up a romance novel with a werewolf in warrior form drawn on the cover. "You've got a much better looking one right here."

Rolling my eyes, I added it to my pile. "I enjoy reading romances."

"She just said we aren't romantic enough for her," Triston said and put a hand to his chest. "I'm so insulted."

"These books set unrealistic expectations," Branson grumbled.

"You all could learn a thing or two from these books," I said, though I didn't really mean it. I'd lucked out with my four mates.

Caleb rolled his eyes, but didn't reply.

I handed Branson the stack. "I'd like these, please."

He nodded and carried them up to the register.

Walking outside, I waved to Lily who was eating a meat stick while sitting on Ezio's shoulders.

She waved her meat stick at me, patted him on the head while saying something, and then nodded at his response.

He went inside the building in front of them and came back out at the same time Branson returned with the bag of books.

Ezio carried over five meat sticks and held them out. "Lily said she wanted you all to try it as well."

"It's yummy!" she shouted and shook hers before taking another big bite.

"Thanks for helping with her, Ezio," I said as I took one from him.

"No problem. I had younger sisters growing up and I help with the pups in the pack all the time. Having an alpha with them helps in a lot of situations." He held up another stick for Lily just as she finished the one in her hand.

She squealed and swapped sticks with him, resuming munching on meat.

"So yummy," she said around the food in her mouth.

As we resumed walking down the street, several people bowed as we passed them on the streets, or as we entered their shops. I still wasn't used to it. Lily giggled each time, clearly enjoying the attention.

We got to a square with a huge fountain and there were several families with children running around. Lily patted Ezio on the top of his head. "Play?"

Ezio looked at me, but I looked at Caleb.

Caleb nodded. "You can play with the children, just remember the rules."

"No shifting. No biting. No be mean. Stay in guards' sight," she repeated.

Ezio set her down. "Go have fun."

She ran over and the children talked to her a moment, she pointed at us, they all looked over at us, their eyes wide, and after a moment, they nodded and let her join in on their game of tag.

"Come, sit," Riddick said and patted an empty bench.

I sat down, sighing as I finally got off my feet for the first time in hours. "Shopping is always tiring," I muttered.

"Would you like me to rub your feet?" Triston offered.

"No, thank you."

He pouted. "Fine."

Rolling my eyes, I said, "Nope, you're not rubbing my feet no matter what puppy dog eyes or tiger eyes you give me. These boots are too time-consuming to lace up." The knee-high boots were gorgeous, comfortable, and it had taken me ten minutes just to lace them up. Leona had given them to me yesterday after she'd done her own shopping trip here.

The families in the square ranged in race, but sadly none were hybrids. One little girl sat at the fountain with her mother and kept stealing glances at me around her mom's arm.

Smiling warmly, I waved at her.

She tapped her mom, pointed, and ran across the square towards me. Her mother walked after her, smiling apologetically as they approached.

The little girl, no older than ten, sported blonde pigtails so light they almost looked white. She bowed to us and when she straightened, she looked at me and said, "Someday, I want to be as strong and beautiful as you, Queen Ember! Thank you for saving us yesterday." She bowed again and ran back to the fountain.

Her mother smiled at me. "We were a few rows back from the bomb when you teleported the man away. She's been talking about you nonstop since then." She bowed and said, "Thank you for protecting us. We will always remember your sacrifice." She looked at Triston. "Thank you for protecting Her Majesty and we are very glad you are safe as well."

He dipped his head to her.

The woman walked back to the fountain where her daughter was talking animatedly with a friend next to them.

"I know we didn't really talk about it, but you did great, Emmy," Caleb whispered and leaned down to kiss the top of my head, leaning his elbows on the back of the bench on either side of me. "Nana Addy told me about you using your shields and your senses. I'm very proud to be such a powerful and smart woman's mate."

Tilting my head upside back so I could look at him almost upside down, I said, "Amos wasn't completely wrong in his accusation that day. It was my fault they were there."

Caleb shook his head. "No, they would have come that day for Riddick and I, even if I'd never found you or accepted my mantle as king. They've been chasing after us for years."

Ezio growled and our eyes whipped back to where Lily was playing.

A group of them were on the ground, piled on each other, but they all froze as he walked over.

He reached into the pile, pulled out a little boy, and set him on his feet. Ezio squatted down and said something to the little boy who wiped blood from his nose and nodded, turned, and dipped his head to Lily.

Lily wiped blood from her own nose and said something to Ezio.

"Should we intervene?" I asked softly.

"No, let Ezio handle it," Caleb said. "I want to see what happens."

A large man stomped over, hands clenched into fists, and pushed the little boy behind him, shouting and pointing at Lily.

Branson started to move forward, but Caleb grabbed his arm. "Just wait."

Ezio slowly stood, faced the man, and said something to him calmly, but sternly.

The man glanced down at Lily and then at the little boy. After a moment, his shoulders relaxed and he held out his hand to Ezio.

Lily held her hand out and she and the little boy shook hands. Lily looked up at Ezio, said something, and he nodded. Immediately, she grabbed the little boy's hand and ran back to play with the other kids.

Ezio walked over and winked. "Just a slight altercation. Everything's fine."

Seeing that interaction definitely had me feeling less hesitant to send Lily to the werewolf school with him as her guard.

"There you lot are," Rhys said behind us.

We spun around and I smiled at the pink summer dress Jolie wore, one I had purchased for her.

Standing, I walked over and hugged her. "That dress looks great on you."

She spun in it and said, "I know! This sweet woman bought it for me. Can you believe it?"

"She clearly has good taste," I said with a nod.

"I don't know who is worse, Mom and Ember or Mom and Leona," Caleb said with a scoff.

"Shut up, you love us," Jolie said and pulled him into a hug.

He patted her back and laughed softly. "Yes, I do. How are you feeling, Mom?"

"Perfectly fine, thank you. I was only knocked out with a sleep spell and cracked my head a tiny bit."

When Jolie had fallen from the spell, the back of her head had hit the concrete stands and cracked. Thankfully, it hadn't been serious.

"Where's my granddaughter?" Fox asked, looking around. He spotted her, shifted into fox form, and ran over to play.

Deryn pulled me into a hug, startling me. "I know Rhys and I have been hard on your during trainings the past few months, but I want you to know how proud we are."

Why was it that these grown adults saying they were proud was about to bring tears to my eyes? They weren't my parents!

Rhys pulled me away from Deryn and hugged me next. "You protected not only us, but everyone in the stands and truly made us proud."

"Thank you," I said and smiled up at both of them. "I'm just glad no one was seriously injured."

"Em! Em!" Lily shouted.

Everyone spun, myself included, to see what she needed.

She pointed at Fox, laying across her lap, and said, "Grandpa Fox is a fox!"

Oh, right, she hadn't seen them in animal forms yet.

Smiling, I nodded.

She ran over and looked up at Rhys. "What are you?"

"Dragon," he answered and shifted his head only.

She gasped and clapped. Spinning to Deryn, she asked, "Wolf?"

He canted his head slightly. "Yes, how could you tell?"

"Wolves are scowl-y," she said and pushed her eyebrows down with her fingers while frowning hard.

Caleb threw his head back as he laughed and Deryn tackled him. "Oh, you think it's funny? I'll show you funny."

The two rolled across the grass and after a moment, shifted into their wolf forms.

Ezio shifted into his wolf form and tackled Deryn away from Caleb.

"Can I fly?" Lily asked Rhys.

He looked down at her and asked, "Fly?"

She nodded and pointed up towards the sky. "Up!"

"Lily, it's not nice to ask to ride people in their shifted form," I told her gently. "It's rude. What if someone asked to hold you in snake form?"

She frowned as she thought about it and looked at Rhys. "Sorry, Papa Rhys."

I swore I saw his heart physically melt as she called him that. He squatted down, grabbed both her tiny hands in his, and asked, "What if I take you flying when you guys come visit us next?"

Her eyes brightened, her mouth dropped, and she nodded happily. "Yes!"

• • •

"She's got them all wrapped around her finger already, hasn't she?" Jolie asked me softly.

I nodded. "Yep."

"Lord help whoever she ends up with," Jolie said with a shake of her head. "That girl is going to be spoiled and won't take less than an uber alpha."

"Or a few of them," I said with a chuckle.

"You think someone exists who won't be terrified of meeting all of the royals when she brings them home the first time?" Jolie asked.

I shrugged. "I didn't think you'd be welcoming, but you were."

"It's different for boys and girls, even if I don't agree with it," she whispered. "I know the men will be overly protective of her."

"Yes, they're going to be incredibly protective. I just hope that we don't spoil her rotten."

Jolie shrugged. "I spoiled Caleb rotten and he still managed to find you."

Rolling my eyes, I shook my head. "He is spoiled rotten."

"Let's get food!" Lily shouted and waved her hand at us from where she stood with Ezio and Rhys.

"Okay," Jolie agreed joyously. "What do you want to eat?"

"Noodles!" Lily exclaimed and raced over to stand before Jolie, hopping from one foot to the other in her excitement.

"The princess has demanded noodles!" Jolie announced. "It shall be so!"

Caleb scooped up Lily and nuzzled her cheek. "Let's go get those noodles, Princess Lily."

"Yeah, you're definitely going to spoil her rotten," I said with a chuckle, and followed after my new family.

CHAPTER TWENTY-TWO

"School day!" Lily shouted as she raced down the stairs, her backpack already on, and the outfit we'd picked out last night on. She slid to a stop in the dining room where we were all already eating breakfast.

"Yes, today is your first day of school, which means you need to eat a good breakfast before you go," I reminded her. I patted the empty seat beside me and she hopped up, immediately beginning to eat the plate that Branson had prepared for her.

"What are your plans for the day?" I asked Riddick.

I was going to the werewolf pack to help with the farm animals. Apparently, several of them had stopped eating and they weren't sure why. Caleb was going with me to talk some things over with Dan about the island and our visit that we left for tomorrow. Branson was going with us to spend time with his werewolf pack friends. Triston had plans with some of our clan, working with them on things we needed done around the property. We weren't giving them much notice, so we had to get as much done so they were ready for our absence.

After the Summit, we'd received calls from a lot more hybrids, and our clan was now over one hundred members strong! Everyone was shocked at how many hybrids we'd located, especially knowing there were likely more out there that hadn't revealed themselves. We knew it would take time to change public perception, but things were already moving in a positive direction.

"I'm going to train with Silverowl today," Riddick answered.

"Don't overwork yourself," I ordered him.

"Pfft, he never does," Caleb said.

Riddick threw his bread roll at Caleb, but Caleb easily caught it and began to eat it.

Lily laughed and asked, "Can we throw food?"

"No," I said quickly. "Riddick is naughty for throwing food."

"Naughty, Rid!" Lily said and shook her finger at him.

"I apologize," Riddick said and dipped his head to her.

Ezio knocked on the front door twice before entering, knowing our door was always open. "Ready to go?"

Lily shoveled her last bite of food into her mouth, nodded, and hopped off her chair to run up to him.

I finished my food, stood, and grabbed my backpack that had lunch, snacks, and treats for the animals. "Yes, we're ready."

Caleb took his time putting his shoes on, earning an eyeroll from Ezio, and Lily hopping from foot to foot anxiously.

"Come on," she whined. "We're going to be late!"

Caleb moved his foot forward slowly. "I feel so heavy! So ... heavy."

She squealed, grabbed his hand, and tried to pull him, grunting with the strain. "Come on! I'm late!"

Caleb slumped forward. "Going to ... fall!"

"Papa!" she screeched.

Laughing, he scooped her up, and ran to the SUV. "Hurry up, Ezio! We're going to be late!"

Lily laughed and looked over Caleb's shoulder. "Mama! Come on!"

Even after a few months of hearing it, it still made my heart soar and brought tears to my eyes.

"I'm coming!" I called back. After giving Riddick and Triston quick kisses, I hurried out to the SUV and the impatient child vibrating in the car seat.

"Let's go!" I shouted and shut the door.

Ezio started the SUV and drove us to the werewolf den. He dropped Caleb off at the main house where he would meet with Dan, drove me to the farm, and then took Lily to her first day of school. Originally, I had wanted to go as well, to see her off, but Caleb had talked me out of it.

Walking up to the barn, I was immediately welcomed by the animals with a chorus of calls.

"Ember!" Winnie squealed from her stall.

I hurried over to pet her first and say hello before moving to the next stall. This stall housed an older pig who was eating less. "Hello, friend," I greeted.

"Weird smell," the pig muttered.

"Yes, I suppose I do smell weird to you. So, can you tell me why you aren't eating?"

"Hurts."

"It hurst to eat?" I asked.

The pig raised its head and looked at me. "You can understand me?"

I nodded.

"Ember's a friend!" Winnie yelled.

The pig huffed. "That one's weird."

I covered my mouth to keep from laughing. "So, when you eat, it hurts?"

The pig snorted. "Yes. Lots of pain."

"Can I look inside of your mouth? I think you might have a tooth that's causing it."

The pig eyed me a moment, but said, "Fine."

Stepping into the stall, I waited as the old pig slowly opened its mouth. I barely had to even look to see the rotted tooth in the back.

"Yeah, you definitely have a bad tooth. I'll let them know so they can get it fixed for you and then it won't hurt to eat anymore."

"Really?" the old pig asked and closed its mouth. "Really?"

I nodded. "Yep. They'll remove that tooth and then you'll eat like you used to."

"*Wow.*"

I patted its shoulder and exited the stall, being sure to lock it up behind me.

The last stop of the day was a little calf was refusing to drink the milk they were providing it. The poor thing's mother had died giving birth to her. "Hello, little one," I crooned. "I'm Ember."

"Ember's nice!" Winnie shouted. "Nice lady!"

"*So thirsty*," the little calf whined. "*Mommy!*"

Taking the bottle out, I said, "I've got some yumminess right here. Take a drink."

The calf huffed, but didn't move, completely ignoring me.

"This will help you feel strong and happy," I promised. "Come on." I climbed over the gate, knelt, and squirted a bit into her mouth.

The calf swallowed it, her eyes widened, and she nudged my knee. "More! More!"

After I ensured she finished the entire bottle, I asked, "Would you like to play with some friends?"

"*Friends?*" she asked and raised her nose up to look at me.

I nodded. "One of my friends is here, a pig who likes to have fun. I know you two would get along great. What do you say? You want to meet her?"

She bobbed her head. "*Yes!*"

Grabbing the lead, I opened her door, lead her out, then opened Winnie's door. "Winnie, come with us," I said.

"*Okay!*" Winnie exclaimed and trotted after us, oinking as she followed.

When I got to one of the empty paddocks with lots of grass, I opened the gate and let them both in, then unclipped the lead from the calf. "Now, you two go play and be nice to each other, okay?"

"*Tag?*" Winnie asked the calf.

"*Tag?*" the calf asked back, confused.

Winnie went into a long explanation, spinning and oinking as she did, but once the calf understood, Winnie bumped her nose against the calf and started trotting around the pen.

I hopped up onto the wooden fence and watched as the calf and Winnie played, both laughing happily.

"Wow," a werewolf woman said as she approached, a pair or dirty overalls on and rubber boots up to her knees. She leaned her arms on the fence and said, "I thought she was a goner. How did you do it?"

"I can communicate with animals," I explained. "So, I thought I would put my powers to good use and help out animals that aren't able to communicate with their owners."

"So, you're an animal psychiatrist?" she asked.

Chuckling, I shrugged. "In a sense, I guess. Really, I'm just a translator."

"Like that kids' book about the veterinarian who could talk to animals," she said with a nod.

"Ah, I am not a veterinarian. I am a healer, but not the best."

She looked at me a moment and then her eyes widened. "Your Majesty! Oh, I'm sorry. I didn't recognize you." She bowed quickly.

"Please, don't fret. I'm not here as a queen. I'm here to help your farm at King Dan's request."

Straightening, she asked, "What's it like going from average citizen to queen? It can't be easy."

Laughing, I shook my head. "No, it definitely hasn't been easy. I'm lucky enough to have a great support system."

"I saw that video of you teleporting that man with the

bomb away. It was truly impressive. Just how powerful are you?"

"Honestly, I'm not sure. I don't really try to measure it. My goal is to become strong enough, know enough spells, and learn enough to keep me and my people safe. That's all that matters to me, keeping everyone I care about safe."

She hopped up onto the fence next to me while nodding. "That's pretty much all of our goal. At least the majority of the people I know. I saw that same drive in Prince Caleb, excuse me, King Caleb, when he was growing up. I've been working on this farm for twenty years and I've watched him during that time. I have definitely noticed an improvement to him and his attitude since you've come around. He was always a good person, played with the kids, visited and treated all of us as equals, but there was an avoidance, a bubble around him that seemed like it was impenetrable. Women tried to approach him and while he was never rude, you could tell he wasn't interested, but he also looked lonely. Now, I can see that you've filled whatever void he felt. I was beginning to worry since he was in his late twenties, but it seems fate was just making you all wait a bit longer than others."

"While I wish I could have met them all sooner, I do think it was for the best. There were many things we needed to experience to be ready for each other," I said softly.

She smiled and looked towards the city. "That's how I feel about my mate. He was so neglected as a child and I wish I could have found him sooner, to help erase some of that, but we cannot change the past, no matter how hard we wish.

The only thing we can do, is make sure they have the brightest future possible."

"What's your name?" I asked.

She held out her hand. "I'm Tanika."

I shook her hand. "It's nice to meet you, Tanika."

"*Ember!*" Winnie yelled. "*She's my new best friend! Can you believe it?*"

"That's great, Winnie!" I yelled back.

Tanika arched a brow. "The pig said that the calf is her new best friend."

Tanika's eyes widened and she looked back at them. "Really? Well, that's good to know. Maybe I can keep them together in the barn until the calf bulks up a bit. What do you think?"

"I'll ask," I said. "Winnie! Do you want to share your stall in the barn with your new best friend?"

"*Yes!*" they both shouted.

Chuckling, I said, "They both unanimously agreed to that suggestion."

"That is truly the coolest thing. You could probably make a ton of money with the best animal show." She paused and said, "Though, I suppose you aren't really hurting for money."

"If I had more free time, that would be something I considered," I said. "Oh, before I forget, the older pig that's not eating has a rotted tooth that needs removed."

She gasped and snapped her fingers. "So, that's what the decay smell was! I knew he didn't smell like he was dying, but could still smell that decay scent. I'll get them to remove the bad tooth tomorrow."

Branson walked across the yard and I raised my hand, waving at him. He raised it back, but instead of coming to see me, he knelt at the fence to greet Winnie, who squealed happily to see him after so long.

"I always wanted to be a bear," Tanika commented. "I knew it wasn't possible, since my parents are werewolves, but I've seen his animal form a few times and it always makes me jealous."

I eyed the muscular woman and said, "You would have made an excellent bear."

"Right!" she exclaimed and shook her head. "If only I'd been a hybrid, it might have been possible."

Someone wishing to be a hybrid … I never thought I'd see the day.

"Hello, beautiful," Branson greeted.

"That's no way to speak to a woman when your mate is right here," Tanika teased.

"Branson, this is Tanika. Tanika this is Branson," I introduced.

They shook hands and he leaned against the fence beside me. "I see the calf is doing better."

I nodded. "Winnie and she are best friends now."

"Makes my job easier," Tanika said. "Thank you again. I really was worried we were going to lose her."

I dug in my pocket and pulled out my cell phone. "We can exchange numbers and anytime you need me, I'll come help."

Her eyes widened, but she took the phone and entered her information, sent herself a message, and saved my number in her phone. "Thank you. I will probably take you up on that."

"Are you done visiting?" I asked Branson.

He nodded. "Are you finished as well?"

I hopped off the fence. "Yes. Should we head to the main house?"

Branson nodded, intertwined our fingers, and lead the way. I waved to Tanika and she waved back.

"Any word on how Lily's doing?" I asked.

He nodded. "I snuck over before I came here."

Of course he had.

"She's doing great. Remember the little boy she played with at the town during the Summit?"

I nodded.

"He goes to school here, so they're already friends and he's introduced her to his other friends."

"Oh, is a love blossoming?" I asked.

Branson growled. "They're too young for that."

Laughing, I patted his arm. "Oh, Branny Boy, you are in for a wild ride with that girl over the next ten years."

"With you as her mom, I don't doubt it."

I poked him in the ribs, making him jerk sideways. "Rude!"

"If the rabbit tail fits!" He turned and ran towards the house, laughing.

"You get back here!" I shouted, shifted into warrior form, and hopped quickly after him.

"That's cheating!" he yelled as he shifted into his warrior form to run faster away from me.

"There's no cheating in love or war and this is both!" I yelled.

CHAPTER TWENTY-THREE

The entire car ride home, Lily talked nonstop about her day and how much fun she'd had. Ezio reported that everyone had seen her on television during the Summit with us, so he really wasn't needed to keep them from bullying her. I was skeptical, but also knew true bullying came when they got older, like eleven years old and above.

We returned to our clan, heading to an area we called the main square, after saying goodbye to Ezio.

With the increase in clan members, we'd had to build a lot more houses, and we'd even built a little store where members could buy items instead of worrying about leaving the territory or ordering things to be delivered.

Dan had ordered his construction crew to build a gazebo in the center of the little city, just in front of the new store, and put some bushes and flowers around it. It was cute and inviting and got used daily. That was our main square and where we met with everyone who was currently there.

Lily ran over to the kids, playing with them.

"Thank you, everyone, for gathering today," Caleb said in greeting as we stopped at the steps of the gazebo to talk to everyone. "We wanted to inform you that we are going to be heading out on a short trip again. We will be provided guards, though, after the incident at the Summit, we hope that they do not end up being necessary."

"How long will you be gone?" Kieran asked.

"Two to four days," I answered. "We aren't sure what we'll find there, so it may be longer than the two days we anticipated. We will take a train and then a boat to and from the island."

"You're going to the island?" Kieran asked with a scowl. "Do you have any idea what's there?"

"Wilderness and wildlife, from what we've been told, but no one has set foot on it in quite a long time," Caleb replied.

"Don't worry about things here," Dominick, one of the first alphas to come after the Summit, said. "We'll keep things safe here." Dominick had one of the most unique animal forms, a gorilla.

Lily was terrified of him and I didn't blame her. He was huge in gorilla form and when you are a small shifter, it's disconcerting to face someone that much larger. Thankfully, he was a gentle giant. Eventually, Lily would warm up to him like she had with Branson.

"Thank you, that makes me feel better," I said and smiled at him.

"If there's anything you need before we leave, please let us know so we can make the necessary arrangements," Triston said.

"More treats!" Arthur, a toddler who shifted into a racoon yelled.

The adults laughed and his mother shook her head at him. "We have treats at home, Arthur."

"More!" he yelled.

Triston pulled off a backpack I hadn't realized he was wearing, pulled out a plastic bag, and opened it to reveal several small packets of jerky. "I happen to have some treats."

Arthur gasped, looked up at his mom, and after she nodded, he, and several other kids, ran over to get a bag. Even Lily ran over.

"Alright, we're going to return to the main house, but let us know if anything comes to mind," Caleb said.

Branson snagged Lily and tossed her up into the air before catching her. He repeated this all the way to the house, and she giggled the entire time.

We had debated for several hours about taking Lily or not. Jolie had even offered to keep her at their house, which would have been a safe space for her. Ultimately, we didn't want to be separated from her, plus Ezio had offered to come with us as her personal guard.

"What's for dinner?" I asked. "I'm starving."

"Riddick is making dinner as we speak," Triston answered.

"Oh, nice. He's a great cook." Whatever he was making, I was certain I would love it.

"I want fish!" Lily shouted.

"Fish?" I asked. "You want fish?"

She nodded. "We had samson at school today and it was really yummy fish!"

"Salmon," Caleb corrected.

"Yes, that!" she said and pointed at his face.

"We aren't having salmon tonight, but it's good to know you like it so we can make it in the future," Branson said. "Salmon is one of my favorites."

"Did you have time to pack at all?" I asked Triston.

"My friends are sad I'm leaving already," Lily commented and pouted. Quickly, the pout turned into a smile. "I promised I'd come back soon, though, and we played tag!"

"Did you learn anything new today?" Branson asked and set her on the porch on her feet.

"Math!" she hissed. "But teacher showed us in a ... fun way."

"Math can be fun?" I teased.

"I didn't think so, but it was fun counting snacks!" she exclaimed.

Ah, that did make sense why she thought it was fun now. She was definitely food motivated.

When I stepped into the house, Riddick pulled me into a gentle hug and kissed my cheek. "Welcome home, Ember."

I hugged him back and tilted my head back to kiss him on the lips. "Thank you. Did you have a good training session with Silverowl?"

He stepped back and nodded. "I did. I'm getting better at using roots to bind someone."

"Oh, nice, that is a really handy one," I commented with a nod. Inhaling, my mouth filled with drool. "What is that delicious smell?" Definitely something with garlic.

"You're probably smelling the garlic bread since I just took it out of the oven. I also made chicken parmigiana."

"Yes!" I shouted and ran to front bathroom to wash my hands. Lily was at my side, up on the step stool we'd put for her, and washed her hands after me. It was one of our rules. Wash your hands before dinner.

We dried our hands off and hurried out to the dining table, sitting in our normal seats. She frowned down at her booster seat. "I don't like this. I'm not a baby."

"It's just so you're able to reach the table better," I said. "It's not for babies."

"Hmph," she said and folded her arms across her chest.

The guys carried out the plates of food and we eagerly dug in. After dinner, Lily and I took a shower, changed into pajamas, and raced downstairs to play a card game with everyone. It had become a weeknight ritual. While they played a second round, I went to my room and finished packing the suitcases for our trip tomorrow.

"Did you think you'd be traveling this often when you left with us?" Riddick asked from behind me.

I shook my head. "I had hoped I would get to travel, but traveling once a month isn't what I expected." We had another trip planned for next month to take Lily to the beach so she could see it for the first time.

"You're nervous," he commented and wrapped his arms around my waist. "Is it about the trip?"

"Yes. We don't know for certain what we are going to find there and that worries me, especially since we're taking Lily."

"You would worry more if she was out of your sight," he reminded me.

Folding up a pair of pajamas, I put them in the suitcase. "Yes, I know."

Turning me around, he pulled me flush against him. "You are a truly beautiful woman, Ember. I can't believe I'm lucky enough to call you my mate."

Tracing a finger along his chiseled jaw, I said, "I'm the lucky one. You're handsome, smart, a great cook ..."

He chuckled.

"... and a loving person who accepted Lily without hesitation. And you make the best garlic bread in the world." Rising up on my toes, I pressed my lips to his.

He kissed me back hungrily, slid a hand into my hair, and tilted my head to get better access. His tongue swept across mine and I became putty in his hands.

Picking me up beneath my butt, he carried me to his room, shut and locked the door behind us, and fell onto the bed, cradling my head as we fell.

Laughing softly, I unbuttoned his shirt while he worked on mine.

"Why did we choose buttons today?" he grumbled when one didn't want to work on my shirt. With a snarl, he jerked the shirt apart, sending buttons flying across the room.

"Good thing I didn't like this shirt," I teased.

He pulled his shirt off and said, "I'll buy you fifty new shirts."

After unbuttoning and unzipping my pants, to ensure he didn't break those, too, I crawled up the bed and lay on my back. "So, what will it be tonight, sir?"

He removed his pants and gripped himself. "At this point, I'd settle for staring at your lovely body while I stroked myself."

Frowning, I crooked my finger. "I would not like to settle for that tonight."

A noise had him tilting his head. "Well, we don't have much time, so sadly, this will need to be quick." Jumping onto the bed, he crawled up my body, dropping kisses along my stomach and between my breasts as he moved. Once positioned over me, he smiled, a dazzling, beautiful smile, and said, "Quick doesn't mean unpleasant, though." He reached down and stroked between my folds, moaning at how wet I was. Pumping his fingers into me quickly, he built the pressure and then right as I was about to orgasm, he removed his fingers and thrust into me. Immediately, I threw my head back and orgasmed. Had we not needed to be quiet, I would have screamed.

Leaning down, he kissed my neck, flicked his tongue across the sensitive skin, and nipped me rapidly, all in time to his thrusts.

"Riddick," I whispered, my fingers digging into his back as I matched his thrusts with my own, adding even more friction and pleasure.

His speed increased and thrusts grew harder. I tried to match him, but as my orgasm hit, I could only hold on and try not to pass out from the pure bliss that shattered me.

He grunted and dropped his head down as he found his own release, our bodies sweaty even from such a short encounter. "Shower time," he whispered and scooped me up.

"Then you get to help me pack," I said.

He sighed dramatically. "I suppose I can help with that next."

Our shower was quick and it only took us another ten minutes to finish packing the suitcases. When we got back downstairs, Lily was already asleep, passed out on the couch while Branson and Triston continued to watch episodes of her favorite show.

"You realize she's asleep, right?" I asked as I sat between them.

"This is a really good show," Branson said.

"The dad's pretending to be one of those claw machines from the arcades and making them do chores around the house to win back their own toys. He's freaking brilliant," Triston said.

I watched the show with them and found myself also engrossed in the short episodes. Caleb joined us a bit later, hair wet from a shower, and asked, "What are you all doing?"

"Shush!" we all shouted and returned to the show, watching an episode that was hitting close to home about me not feeling like a good enough mom.

"Why is everyone crying?" Lily asked as she sat up and rubbed her eyes.

"Come on, cub, it's bedtime," Caleb said and scooped her up. She shivered and tried to burrow into him. "Do you want the bed or the hot rock?"

Since she was a snake, we'd done our research and found that they often liked warm rocks to sleep on, so Caleb had had a large one designed and built inside of her room.

"Rock," she said and shifted into her snake form, curling around his arm with her head resting on his open palm.

"She's so cute when she curls around your arms like that," I whispered.

"Speaking of cute," Branson said and picked me up in a bridal carry. "It's also your bedtime."

"I don't want to," I whined in an overexaggerated tone. "I'm not sleepy."

He rolled his eyes. "Your head is going to hit that pillow and you're going to pass out."

"Says the one who will be snoring faster than I can even get into the bed," Triston countered.

"Hey, we're not talking about me," Branson growled.

"Does someone have an alarm set for tomorrow?" I asked and yawned.

"Yes, Riddick and Caleb both have alarms," Triston answered, and yawned. "Dang it! You're making me yawn."

"It's not my fault they're contagious," I mumbled. My eyes were growing heavier the farther up the stairs we went, so I leaned my head against Branson's chest and closed my eyes. "Thanks, Branny Boy."

"Anything for you, Em."

"Even truffle hunting?" I asked. I'd forced him to go with me truffle hunting one day and he'd sworn never to do it again.

"Anything, but that," he whispered back, making me laugh.

CHAPTER
TWENTY-FOUR

We were once again almost late to the train, but made it in time, earning a side eye from the man who checked our tickets.

The train ride was only a few hours, so we sat in the glass car to watch the scenery.

Lily watched with wide eyes, pointing at things and making Ezio look for them. He got her to play I-spy and she had so much fun that we had to stop the game to get her to eat lunch.

Two mammoth-sized men with identical faces and long beards met us at the train station, bowing to us as we walked.

"Hello, I'm Stan," the one on the left said, his voice the deepest I had ever heard a human speak.

"I'm Clark," the other said, his voice just as deep as his twin's. "We will drive you to the boat, which we will be taking and we will operate the vessel as well."

"It's nice to meet you," I greeted.

"Good to see you two again," Ezio said and held out his fist so they could bump theirs against it.

"You look well," Stan said.

"Thanks for your assistance today," Caleb said and hugged each of them.

"Of course, Caleb. You know you can always call on us," Clark said and patted his back. He looked over at me and said, "I hope he's not giving you too much trouble as a mate."

"I'm a perfect mate," Caleb said and scoffed.

"Ha! I could smell that lie in a manure factory," Stan said and ruffled Caleb's hair.

"Everyone, put the luggage in the back and get into the SUV or we'll be here all day," Ezio ordered. "These two love teasing Caleb."

"He's got such a teasable face," Clark said and pinched Caleb's cheek.

Caleb growled and said, "You're lucky we've got places to be or I'd shift and show you who's alpha here."

"I'm shaking in my fur," Clark said mockingly.

Once buckled, we headed away from the city and towards the ocean. We rolled down the windows, letting the salty air fill our nostrils.

"What's that smell?" Lily asked, wrinkling her nose.

Stan looked at us in the rearview mirror. "She's never seen the ocean?"

I shook my head.

"Can she swim?" Clark asked.

We all looked at Lily who nodded. "I love water and it's very easy to swim in animal form."

Oh, right. Snakes were excellent swimmers.

"What animal is she?" Clark asked, turning from the passenger seat to look at us.

"Can't tell you," Lily whispered and ducked her head down.

"You don't have to hide your animal form anymore," I told her. "Remember, you aren't hiding anymore."

Her eyes widened and she looked up at Clark. "Snake."

Now his eyes widened. "Snake?"

"Yes, she's a snake," I answered. "Apparently, there was only one snake before her in all of elven history."

"Interesting," Clark said. He looked at Branson. "What are you?"

"Bear," Branson replied while still looking out the window of the SUV.

"You?" Clark asked Triston.

"Tiger."

"Bear, tiger, cheetah, snake ... what about you?" he asked me.

"Rabbit," I replied with a wide smile.

"Well, that's quite a combination," Stan said and chuckled.

"Do you get to choose your form?" Clark asked.

We all shook our heads.

"Hm, I think I'd want to be a hippo," Clark said as he turned around.

Lily laughed. "A hippo?"

"They're dangerous animals. They can run fast on land and are quick in the water. They may look big and slow, but they are not!" he shuddered, making it clear he had had a run in with a hippo at some point in his life. "Do you know of any hippo shifters?" he asked, looking back at me.

I shook my head. "None of our members are hippos that I know of."

"Stop pestering my mate with questions," Caleb said from the backseat where he was laying back with his eyes closed. "She's not your personal encyclopedia of hybrids."

"Well, you never answer any questions we ask," Stan said. "So, we have to ask someone else."

"Maybe it's because he doesn't know," Clark said. "Maybe she's the one who knows and he's embarrassed that he doesn't know the answers."

"Believe what you want, but stop pestering her," Caleb said and lifted his lip in a snarl.

"Papa's grumpy," Lily whispered.

"Do you have anyone who can take multiple forms, like Caleb?" Clark asked me, clearly ignoring Caleb's order.

"I can take all of my mates' forms," I said, "but I don't know of an unmated person who can take multiple forms aside from Caleb. I think it's because he was magically created to be the perfect hybrid."

"See, she thinks I'm perfect," Caleb said.

Rolling my eyes, I continued, "To be honest, we're still learning a lot about hybrids ourselves since we've been scattered and remained hidden for so long. I didn't even know I was a hybrid until I met Caleb."

"What?" Stan and Clark asked simultaneously.

"I had never shifted into an animal form and thought I was just a mage," I explained. "Caleb sensed I was a hybrid though when we met and that's how I found out."

"So, you think it's possible there are others like you out there?" Stan asked.

"There's no one else like her out there," Caleb said, leaned forward, and kissed my cheek. "She's one of a kind."

"I love you, too," I said and turned to kiss him on the lips.

"Ew!" Lily yelled and covered her eyes.

That made everyone laugh.

They asked me a few more questions as we drove, the drive was over two hours long, so it did help pass the time. Eventually, Caleb started answering some questions I didn't know the answers to.

When the ocean finally came into view, Lily sat up straighter and gasped, "Look at all the water!"

"How long will the boat ride take?" I asked. I had never been on a boat and I wasn't really looking forward to being on the ocean. I had basic knowledge about the types of creatures that lived in the water and a rabbit was not meant for swimming in the ocean.

"An hour and a half," Stan answered.

"Oof," I whispered and felt my heart start to beat faster.

Caleb set his hand on my shoulder and squeezed. "Don't worry, you'll be safe. You can always use my dragon side to give yourself wings, remember?"

Right, I could give myself wings. I kept forgetting about doing that.

"Lily can swim Mama to safety," she said and set her hand on top of mine on my leg. "You be okay."

Now I felt bad for being scared and being reassured by my five-year-old daughter.

"Thanks, Lily," I said and squeezed her against my side.

"Pretty sure you could just shift into rabbit form and sit atop Branson's head while he swims and the extra weight wouldn't bother him," Triston said with a chuckle.

"He's not wrong," Branson mumbled, his eyes were closed and he was relaxed in the seat, looking like he was trying to nap.

"Good to know," I said.

We made it to the dock where a ship awaited us. The men took the luggage, so I carried Lily and followed Clark onto the ship.

When I set Lily on her feet on the ship, she spread her legs wide and gripped me tightly. "Whoa," she whispered.

Yeah, I wasn't really liking the wobbly way the boat moved atop the water either.

"Here, you can sit on the bench here," Clark said and waved us towards a bench in front of the cabin where the wheel was to steer the ship.

Lily and I sat down and waited for everyone to get on and for them to steer the ship out to sea.

Branson sat next to Lily, and she immediately shifted into snake form and curled around his arm.

Triston sat beside me and I leaned against him, resisting the urge to do the same as Lily, shift and be held by them.

Being surrounded by nothing, but water that had creatures capable of eating me was terrifying.

Caleb stood at the front of the ship, breathing the sea air deeply, and looked more at peace than I had ever seen him before.

The guys seemed to sense my unease, so they did not try to talk and we stayed silent the entire trip.

A few sharks approached the ship, but one look from Caleb and they dove back beneath the water without getting too close.

We arrived to the island without issue, but found the dock there in such a terrible state that we knew we couldn't use it.

Clark steered the ship as close as he could and anchored it. Caleb flew to the beach and they started throwing the luggage to him.

Once all luggage was on the beach, Caleb returned to carry a few of us at a time to the beach next.

Turning my back to the sea, I looked at the jungle of trees before us. It was thick, lush, and full of animals calling to each other.

"You sure about this?" Clark asked as he eyed the jungle. "We have no idea what's in there."

"I'm here, so it'll be okay," Caleb said confidently. "Let's make a temporary shelter to store the luggage, ensuring it's safe from waves or creatures nearby, and then we'll head in."

They used vines and tree branches to make a platform that hung from one of the trees and put all of our luggage inside. I put my backpack with healing and medical supplies on and Branson put on his pack that had food and water. Triston and Ezio also had water and food rations in their bags and Ezio had emergency clothing for Lily.

Caleb turned to me. "Ember, you walk behind me. Ezio, you and Lily stay in the center of us. The rest of you, make a protective circle around the girls."

Everyone nodded and we headed into the jungle.

Lily stayed in her snake form, but coiled up around his

neck, raising up to look around as we walked. She was clearly more comfortable in this environment than most of us, except for Triston.

"I feel ... at home," he whispered and shook his head. "This place really calls to my beast side."

"Not mine," I whispered.

"Well, since most things here could kill a rabbit, that makes sense," Riddick said behind me.

I spun to glare at him. "Not helping."

Caleb held up his hand and everyone froze. Tilting his head back, he sniffed the air. "Show yourself," he called out. "We mean you no harm."

Stepping from the trees before us was a huge black panther and just behind the panther slithered an at least twenty-foot-long green python. I felt the pull towards them ... hybrids.

Lily perked up more, but Ezio shook his head and she stilled.

"I am Caleb, King of Hybrids. Who are you?" He spoke politely and I could tell was holding back his aura.

The panther shifted into a male warrior form, a combination of man and panther, with beautiful dark skin and hair in thick, braided rows. "King? You do not seem strong enough to be king."

Caleb smiled. "I didn't want to let my aura out to ensure you didn't view me as menacing. I am here as a friend, not enemy."

"Prove your status as king," the python said as she shifted into a snake-woman form. Her green scales still covered most of her body and she kept a few feet of tail behind her.

Caleb inhaled and as he exhaled, his aura pressed down upon us all.

Thankfully, as part of the clan and his pack, it didn't affect us much, but I saw Clark and Stan flinch a step away and their shoulders hunch a bit.

The panther and python dropped to a knee and bowed. "Your Majesty," they both gasped.

"Please, stand," Caleb said as he subdued his aura again. "We weren't certain who or what we might find here. I'm excited to find more hybrids. How many of you are there?"

"Twenty," the panther answered.

My eyes widened. Twenty hybrids lived here?

He stood and held out his hand. "I am Paul. This is my mate, Mercy."

She dipped her head to us. "It is a pleasure to meet more hybrids."

"This is my mate and queen, Ember," Caleb introduced and held his hand back for me.

I stepped forward and smile. "Hello."

"Please, follow us and we will take you to our pack," Mercy said and started leading the way.

Paul waited for Caleb and asked, "What is the status of things over there? Are we still persecuted?"

"Things have changed recently," Caleb said with a smile. "We are accepted by most now and we have our own lands, including this island."

Paul frowned. "Someone owned this island?"

Caleb nodded. "My grandfather, King of Werewolves."

Paul's eyes widened. "You are the perfect hybrid?"

Caleb nodded again.

Glancing at me, Paul asked, "And the rest of our pack?"

"We're hybrids as well, except for the three werewolves who accompanied us as additional guards," I answered.

Mercy glanced over her shoulder at Lily. "How old is that one?"

"Five," I answered.

"She is not yours biologically," she said as a statement.

"No, she is our adopted daughter," Caleb answered.

Mercy nodded. "We have many orphans as well in our pack. We raise them as a unit instead of assigning individual families. It makes things easier on the island."

"Are there a lot of dangers here?" I asked. Sure, predators were an issue, but they weren't just animals, so they could create defenses to help keep them at bay. Couldn't they?"

"We will talk more when we are at our village," Paul said and Mercy turned back around, her lips in a thin line.

What had them both so scared?

CHAPTER TWENTY-FIVE

Their village was deep within the forest, had tall wooden walls, and guards that patrolled the walls.

It was a beautiful village of A-frame buildings made from the jungle trees and with some dark substance that looked like mud or clay applied in the grooves that likely kept the rain out.

A thick gate was pulled open by two men, both as large as Stan and Clark.

Where did all these giant men come from? Why were they so big? Was it something they ate or were they just genetically blessed?

The hybrids approached cautiously. There were a couple children, but most were in their twenties or older.

"Everyone, please gather!" Mercy yelled.

Paul set his hand on Caleb's shoulder and said, "Our king has come!"

The cheer that rose surprised me. They were so excited, but they hadn't known about us before, had they?

"We're saved! He's come to save us!" one of the children yelled as he danced around some of the other members.

Saved?

"I think we need to be brought up to speed," Caleb said to Paul.

Paul rubbed the back of his neck and nodded. "Let's take a seat."

We followed him towards a huge bonfire area with logs for seating and took seats on them. The children tried to get close to Lily, but Ezio snarled at them and they ran to hide behind some women.

Lily shifted into her human form and glared at Ezio. "Why you snarl?"

"We don't know them or know if they might harm you," he whispered.

"What is it that you're all so afraid of?" I asked bluntly. "It's not just animals on the island."

"There's a trio of men; we thought they were mages, but they have dark, terrible powers," Paul answered. "If we get caught by them, they curse us and turn us against each other. We haven't found a way to break the curse or return the people to normal."

Mercy ducked her head and sniffled.

Paul set a hand on her shoulder, squeezed, and said, "We've had to kill a few of our own."

"Did they drip black ooze?" I asked, feeling an awful, sinking feeling.

Every set of eyes from the village turned to me.

Paul stood and growled. "How did you know that? How could you possibly have known that?"

Caleb waved his hand, but didn't stand or react aggressively. "Sit down, we aren't the enemy here."

Paul slowly sat.

"I used to live in a forest and mages started cursing animals and shifters to come after me," I explained.

Paul and Mercy looked at each other before turning back to me. "One of them disappeared about a year ago. We thought he had died."

"That was likely him then," I said with a nod. "But why? And how did they know about me?" I turned to Caleb.

This mystery made no sense. We'd thought it was just that mage council, but was it more than that?

"We need to capture one of them," Riddick said. "We need to know who their leader is. Who is ordering them to do this to the hybrids and how they found out about Ember before we did."

Caleb tapped his chin in thought as he stared at the fire before us.

"They are too powerful to be caught," Mercy said and shuddered. "We have a few mages here, but we have never been able to stand against them. The walls are warded, and that's the only way we can keep them out."

"I can trap them," Caleb said. "It would be easier if Dad was here, but I can do it."

"You're talking about using a containment circle, aren't you?" Riddick asked.

Caleb didn't respond.

"Last time you did that, you almost killed yourself."

"I was ten last time I tried in front of you," Caleb countered. “I’m a bit more powerful and have practiced a lot more since then.”

“You’ve been practicing in secret?” Riddick asked, eyes wide.

Caleb looked at me and smiled. “When I realized our wonderful mate was up to such devious things, I started doing them as well.”

Rolling my eyes, I turned to Mercy and Paul again and asked, “Do you have a place we could sleep while we wait for them to come?”

They both nodded.

“We should get our luggage first,” Branson said.

“Ember, Lily, Branson, and Ezio, stay here,” Caleb ordered as he stood. “We’ll go get the luggage and return.”

“You’re splitting the party,” I snapped as I stood quickly.

Caleb hugged me. “It will make me feel better to know you and Lily are safe in the wards here. Now that I’ve been here, I can teleport us if anything happens.”

Gnawing on my lip, I nodded. Even though I didn’t like it, I knew he could handle himself. I just didn’t like being away from him.

He kissed me and pressed his forehead to mine. “We’ll be back soon. Don’t fret.”

We watched them leave, Paul going with them. It was up to me now.

“If danger comes, please gather together and I’ll use a shield,” I informed Mercy.

She frowned. “Shield?”

In demonstration, I formed a shield around myself. “It deflects physical and magical attacks.”

She tapped it and her eyes widened when she met resistance. "Remarkable."

Dropping the shield, I turned to Lily. "What are the rules?"

"Danger, stay with Ezio. If Ezio hurt and everyone fighting, run and hide in snake form."

I smiled wide. "Perfect."

It had only been minutes since Caleb and the others left and yet I felt certain we were going to be attacked while they were gone. What was it? Staring quietly out into the trees, I realized what it was that I sensed.

Branson frowned. "You seem certain they're going to get attacked."

"I can sense malice approaching," I admitted.

Mercy's eyes widened. "You can sense emotions?"

"My bloodline includes sirens, so I can sense emotions. They're nearing, but I can't tell exactly the distance. Malice can be felt farther than other emotions."

"Everyone, they're nearing! Gather here!" Mercy shouted.

Heading towards the wall, I climbed up to the top so I could stand atop it and watch.

Two hooded figures stepped from the trees, but paused when they noticed me.

I created a shield around everyone who stood near the bonfire.

"Ember!" Branson roared.

"What is your purpose?" I asked the mages.

Their hooded heads turned towards each other briefly before turning back to me again.

It irritated me not to be able to see their faces. Why were they hiding their faces?

"Queen of the Hybrids, give yourself to us and we will spare the village," the one on the right said in a strangely lyrical, male voice.

"Mama!" Lily called out.

"Why do you want me? What do you hope to accomplish by taking me?" We needed to better understand their goal to figure out who they were and how to combat them.

"Your blood and the King's blood are the key. We need to know why," the one on the left said, a feminine voice that was raspy, like she'd had a throat injury or something.

"You're experimenting on the hybrids with the curse, why?" I asked. "What are you hoping you will accomplish with these experiments?"

"Come with us and we will show you," the man said. His lyrical tone bothered me. Was he part siren? Was he trying to lure me into using it? Did he not know I was part siren as well?

"Where will you take me?" Did they have a stronghold on the island or were they teleporting somewhere else?

"Our base," the woman answered.

"Ember," Branson growled. "Don't you even think about it."

"Decide!" the man and woman shouted.

Hands on my hips, I glared down at them. "How dare you raise your voice to me when I've been nothing, but polite even though you're traitors and deserve death. I will not stand for this disrespect any longer. Bow before me!" I thrust my hand out and used my connection to

Caleb and through him, Nico, to grip the mages before me.

They dropped to their knees with grunts, straining and fighting against me.

The shield behind me dropped and Branson advanced on them, hopping over the wall to approach them.

"Stop," I ordered him. "They aren't submitting and might break free."

Branson halted, shifted into warrior form, and waited for my command.

Mercy and Ezio, with Lily on his shoulder, joined me on the wall.

"How are you doing this?" Mercy asked.

"Mate bond that connects me to the Mage King," I explained and grunted. "Branson, back up." I jumped down to join him. "I have to release the hold."

He nodded and stood at my side.

Releasing my hold on them, I immediately put a shield up that surrounded not just Branson and I, but Ezio, Lily, and Mercy behind us as well.

"You're too dangerous," the woman said. "We must know what it is about your blood that protects you."

"Come with us or we will murder every hybrid on this island," the man threatened.

"Come get me," I challenged and shifted into my warrior form.

"Bunny tail," Lily giggled behind me.

My mouth twitched as I held back a smile.

The mages got to their feet and started whispering while moving their hands in a weird pattern.

"Mama!" Lily yelled, her voice full of fear.

I turned my head and gasped.

Ezio had fallen off the wall and was on the ground behind me, convulsing.

Lily stood before him, but looked at me uncertainly.

"Come here," Branson ordered her.

Ezio jerked upright on his knees, threw his head back, and howled.

The hair on my nape stood on end.

"They've cursed him," Mercy hissed.

How were they cursing him without touching him or using the stones? Had they improved their spells from using it on so many during the time they were trying to kill me?

"Branson, protect Lily. I'm going to cure him," I said. "Dropping shield in three ..."

He ran to Lily.

"... two, one." Running to Ezio, I changed my right hand into a cheetah's paw and used my claw to cut my arm. Before I could get the blood onto his face, he shifted into warrior form and swiped his claws at me.

I danced backwards, using my rabbit-human legs to jump out of the way quickly, but his claws still cut a bit into my cheek.

Ezio was one of the strongest alphas in the werewolf clan. I wasn't sure I stood a chance against him without the intent to kill him.

"Stop!" Lily screamed, tears flowing down her face.

Ezio leapt towards her and a combination of fear and protective instincts took over.

I changed my right hand back to a human hand, smeared

my fingers in the blood dripping down my opposite arm, and leapt onto Ezio's back. Wrapping my arm around his throat, I wiped the blood over Ezio's mouth and held on while he tried to throw me off and tried to move forward to attack Lily.

Ezio would never forgive himself it he hurt her.

Branson stepped in front of Lily and shoved Ezio in the chest, making him stumble backwards.

The blood was on his lips, but he had to ingest it for it to cure him.

"Lick your lips!" I shouted into his ear and tightened my hold on his throat, trying to cut off his air supply.

Branson swept his leg out, knocking Ezio off balance and making him open his mouth.

I shoved my still bloodied fingers into his mouth and across his tongue, gasping in relief when I pulled my fingers free before his teeth clamped down.

He stopped attacking and dropped to the ground on his hands and knees.

"Inconceivable!" the male mage yelled.

"I'm okay," Ezio panted.

"Bran Bran!" Lily yelled.

His body convulsed and he started to turn towards her.

No. No, they were not going to hurt my mate or my daughter!

As I ran by him, I smeared my blood on his mouth, my eyes focused on the mages. I shifted my hands into cheetah's paws again and swiped at their faces.

Their hoods fell back and I gasped at the faces of my adopted parents.

"How?" I screamed as I continued trying to cut them, my claws tearing their cloaks to shreds. "We killed you!"

"You killed our clones," my adoptive mother said. She clapped her hands together and a powerful wave of wind knocked me backwards.

"We knew you were unique, but we never imagined you were a hybrid. Had we known, we would have kept you and used your blood. Our research would have been so much better if we'd had your blood this whole time."

We battled back and forth with magical attacks as well as my physical ones, and I felt my powers weakening. Branson leapt forward and distracted my adoptive father, attacking him while I attacked my adoptive mother. We had to end this soon or my power would be depleted.

The realization hit me and I cursed myself mentally for not realizing it sooner. "You morons!" I hissed. "You really don't get it, do you?"

"Tell us, brilliant *Daughter*," my adoptive father snapped and hit me with a fire spell that burned my face.

"Hybrids are more powerful and my siren blood protects me from your attempts at emotional manipulation. Your curses are emotion-based. You give the cursed person or creature an emotional desire and my siren blood filled with my desire to put them at peace breaks your curse."

Both of their eyes widened and their momentary hesitation gave me the opportunity to attack my father, my claws burying into his stomach. With a twist, I jerked them out and he dropped to his hands and knees.

My adopted mother screamed, her hands moving in a

circular pattern, and a strange purple and cyan blue, almost oil slick type of color grew.

A terrible feeling had me jumping back to try to avoid the magic. I tugged on my connection to Caleb, but wasn't certain he would arrive in time.

"No, you will not escape this!" she bellowed. "This ends here!" The ball of power in her hands grew larger and larger.

Branson grabbed me and I tried to create a shield, but it didn't fully form, my powers weak.

She threw the power at us and an almost certain feeling of death filled me. There was nothing I could do.

"No!" Lily screamed.

My terror increased as Lily ran between the power and us, her little arms spread wide, and she screamed as the ball of oil slick colored power hit her.

CHAPTER TWENTY-SIX

"Lily!" I screamed and dove towards her.

The power hit her little body and she closed her eyes.

In fear and amazement, we watched as the power absorbed into her, her body glowed with an odd purplish light, and her hair changed color to match the power, becoming streaked with purple and cyan blue.

She started to fall and I caught her in my dive, her body still radiating the power.

"How!" my adoptive mother screamed. "No!"

Caleb teleported with the others beside us and he took a split second to assess the scene before grabbing my adoptive mother in chains he created from the ground, and bound her in them. "What have you done?" he roared in her face. "What is that power?"

"She shouldn't have been able to absorb it," she whispered. "What kind of monster are you hybrids? You're all monsters!"

Cradling Lily in my lap, I stroked her sleeping face with my hand. "Lily, wake up. Please, sweetheart, wake up." Her heart beat and she breathed slowly, but her body was almost burning me to touch it.

Ezio crawled to us in his wolf form, whining, and bumped his nose against her hand that lay limply at my side.

"She's alive," I whispered.

"What was that power?" Caleb demanded.

"A curse to permanently alter personalities," she said.

No! No, Lily can't have absorbed that to protect us. What had it done to her?

"Lily," I said and gently shook her. "Wake up, Lily."

She groaned and her eyelids fluttered open. "Mama?" she asked and whined. "Body hurts."

Hugging her against my chest, I sobbed softly. "I'm so sorry, Lily."

"No cry," she said and patted my back, her voice muffled as I hugged her.

Leaning back, I pulled a strand of her now magically-colored hair forward and showed her. "Your hair changed."

She gasped and pulled as much of her hair forward as she could to look at it. "Pretty!" she squealed, stood, and danced in a circle while looking at her hair. "It's so pretty."

Well, at least she was happy about it.

"How do you feel?" I asked her.

She stopped dancing, pushed her hair back, and said, "Hungry."

"How?" my adoptive mother shouted. "How did she absorb it without it changing her?"

"Lily feels the magic inside," Lily said and patted her

chest. "It's warm and ..." she thought about it a moment, "... angry, but Lily's not angry. She's happy and has happy family."

"Who else are you working with?" Caleb asked my adoptive mother.

She shook her head. "We were the last." Looking at her dead companion, the man I had once called dad, she sobbed. "We were the last. We were so close to finding a way to permanently destroy hybrids. If only we'd had more time. More resources. More of her blood." She looked at me with such hatred that I cringed back.

"I'm going to teleport her to the mage prison," Caleb informed me. He waved Lily towards him and she obediently skipped over. Squatting down, he hugged her with one arm while the other one still held my adoptive mother in the chains. "When we get home, we'll have Great Nana Kara check you over, okay?"

"I'm okay, Papa," she said and patted his shoulder. "The magic doesn't hurt. Promise."

He scowled and I could tell he felt the same as me, even more concerned for her. "Stay with Mama and no more jumping in front of strange magic, okay?"

She giggled. "Okay, Papa."

Ezio picked her up and tapped his finger against the end of her nose. "You're so naughty. Wasn't the rule to stay back and let us protect you?"

"Ezio was in pain," she grumbled. "And ..." her little eyes filled with tears, "... I didn't want to lose another Mama."

He hugged her so tight she squeaked, but she let him continue to hug her.

"Come on, let's get back inside the walls and wards," Branson said, and picked me up in a bridal carry. "Your magic is depleted, my queen."

"I won't be the last," my adoptive mother shouted. "Others will come."

"And we'll defeat them as well," I said without looking at her, letting Branson carry me. "Together, the hybrids will stand and defeat all who oppose us. Just like we defeated you and the H.E."

She sobbed quietly and Caleb teleported them away.

Clark and Stan followed us inside, frowning hard.

Once we were at the bonfire, Branson set me on one of the logs and took a water bottle out of his pack for me.

Lily jumped out of Ezio's arms and ran up to the kids, who all approached and took turns examining her hair. Once they had all expressed their awe, they ran around us playing tag, the horror and drama forgotten.

I wished to be able to live a life like that.

"Eat," Triston ordered me and put a bag of jerky in my lap.

"Are you okay?" I asked Ezio as he sat next to me, eating and drinking as well.

He nodded. "You cured me before the curse could full take effect. Thank you. I felt an urge to kill you all and was fighting it, but I'm not sure what would have happened if you hadn't acted so quickly." He glanced at Lily. "It was terrifying to think it could force me to harm her."

I set my hand on his shoulder and squeezed. "We've experienced this a few times before. I'm glad I could cure you before something happened."

"I know I'm a werewolf and not part of your clan, but call me anytime and I will come." Looking over at Lily where she was wrestling with another little girl, he added, "Especially if it concerns her."

"It sets my nerves a bit to know that she has people like you who will be there for her … if anything should happen."

Riddick growled at me as he sat down on my right side. He linked our hands together and rubbed his face against mine. "You scared me again."

"I'm sorry," I whispered.

"I still can't believe they had clones," he whispered. "That's terrifying to consider."

"What if there are more?" I asked.

"Then we will take care of them when we find them. No need to worry about something that may not come to pass," Caleb said as he teleported back behind us. He pushed Ezio over so he could take the spot beside me. "You sure you're okay?"

I nodded and leaned my head against his shoulder.

Paul and Mercy sat across from Caleb and I.

"You can return with us and live in our clan's territory," Caleb said. "Or, you can stay here since this is also part of our territory. The decision is completely up to you."

"The mages are gone?" Mercy asked.

We both nodded.

"They called you, 'daughter,'" Mercy whispered.

"They were my adoptive parents, but they abandoned me when I was young, sending me to a boarding school, and then they gave me a house in the woods, never talking to me. It wasn't until recently that I learned they were in charge of the Hybrid Eradication organization. We'd thought we killed them, but apparently it was their clones. Now, they won't be able to hurt us ever again."

"We don't know much about the outside world," Paul said. "I'm not sure we would do well there."

"You could come live on our clan lands, learn from the others of our clan, and slowly acclimate yourselves," I suggested. "We could talk to the Werewolf King about your kids going with Lily to the werewolf school, too."

Paul and Mercy looked at each other and frowned.

"You don't have to decide right now," Caleb advised. "We wanted to give you the option so you can discuss amongst yourselves and decide. Also, are we still able to stay the night?" He looked up at the darkening sky.

"Of course," Paul said immediately. "We're going to help with food. Please excuse us."

"Thank you," Caleb said.

Lily ran over to us and asked, "Can we stay the night?"

"Yes," Caleb nodded.

She gasped, spun, and shouted, "They said yes!"

The kids all cheered and she ran back to play with them.

"She seems okay," I whispered, "but I'm still worried."

"Same," he whispered.

"A curse to alter your personality," I whispered. "It sounds more like a siren's ability than a mage's."

"I was thinking that, too," Caleb said and leaned his elbows on his knees then set his chin in his hands. "Perhaps we should speak to Auntie Leona."

"Agreed."

"Although I am worried about Lily, I am really glad that it

didn't hit you," he said and turned to look at me. "I'm not quite sure what I would have done if you went on a rampage. I'm not sure I could stop you."

Smiling, I asked, "Are you flirting with me, sir? Because that type of compliment really goes to a girl's head."

He brushed a kiss across my temple. "Speaking the truth. You are extremely powerful. Not just from your own power, but from being able to harness our powers as well. Plus, there are limits to how much you can do when you don't want to kill someone."

Riddick pulled me against his side and asked, "Can you stop getting into trouble when I'm not with you?"

Chuckling, I snuggled into him closer and kissed his cheek. "I'll try."

"I understand now why Rhys and Jolie's other mates were always stressed when not with her," he whispered. "The thought that your mate could be in trouble and you're too far away to help is terrifying."

"Let's hope we've had enough terrifying for the rest of our lifetime," I said and yawned.

"Come on, let's get you to bed," Triston said and held a hand out for me to take.

Caleb stood. "Yes, it is getting late." He looked over at Lily sleeping on a blanket next to the bonfire with the other children. Her hair was no longer glowing, but seemed like it was going to remain purple and cyan. "I think we can leave our little savior here with her friends for the night."

"I agree," I said with a nod. "She's earned some bonding time with the other children."

Caleb put his arm around my shoulders, leaned his head

down until his lips were right beside my ear, and said in a lower voice, "You've earned bonding time as well."

A shiver of delight went up my spine. "Well, let's not delay any further."

He chuckled and nipped my earlobe. "As you wish, my queen."

EPILOGUE

After a ton of tests and discussion, it was determined that Lily was not in danger and Leona did know of the curse. She advised that we would just need to keep an eye on her moods as she grew up and help her learn to control them if they did get out of control.

The island hybrids decided to live on clan lands for a month and then return to the island. They didn't want to give up their home, but did want to learn more about the world they'd been isolated from.

Lily made fast friends with the island hybrid children, and when they came to visit she immediately took her role as princess seriously. She ensured the other children didn't tease them or bully them and one of the island boys was already enamored with her.

Ezio came over so often that we built a house near ours for him. Dan didn't seem to mind that we'd basically stolen one of his strongest alphas. In fact, he seemed rather happy to know Ezio was there to help add protection to Lily.

It was also becoming obvious that Ezio and one of the island hybrid women were spending quite a bit of time together and it wasn't just when he was watching over Lily.

There were always trials and problems, people who still didn't approve of hybrids and our existence. There was often a fight or battle, but no matter what happened, we had each other.

Lily begged her new fathers to train her and threw herself into the training with determination.

At ten years old, she was already adept at using a shield, and with Mercy's help had learned the best way to take on a warrior form that utilized her snake form that was the most advantageous. We had no doubt that she would eventually surpass us in her skill. In fact, we were looking forward to it.

"Mama!" Lily yelled, pulling me out of my focus on the computer screen before me.

Closing the laptop, I smiled at the rambunctious ten-year-old. "Yes, Lily?"

"It's time to go to Nana Jolie's," she announced. "Papas already packed up the car with the presents and everything."

"Okay, let me put my shoes on," I said, and headed towards the front door with her following close behind.

"Do you think they left the star for me to put on the Christmas tree like I asked?" she asked me softly.

"I'm sure Nana Jolie left the star topper for you just like you asked," I said with a nod. In fact, I knew it for certain as I'd made sure to text her about it a few days ago.

She squealed and danced in a circle. "Yay!"

"Where's your brother?" I asked.

"Bran Bran has him," she answered. "He was being

cranky and didn't want to go into the car seat yet, so he was holding him."

Of course he was. Branson was the quickest to get wrapped around our children's fingers.

We headed out to the SUV where all my mates waited. Branson held our tiny three-year-old son, Anthony, in his arms, bouncing him gently and cooing.

"I'm here!" I announced. "Sorry, I got wrapped up in work again."

Caleb sighed and shook his head. "Weren't you supposed to *not* work during the holidays?"

"Well, technically the holiday part doesn't start until we get to your mom's," I said with a shrug.

Branson buckled Anthony into his car seat and climbed in to sit beside him.

I took the passenger seat while Riddick took the driver's seat. Everyone else piled into the back.

"Ready?" I asked.

"Yes!" Lily shouted and raised her hands in the air with a wide smile.

Anthony cooed, which I took as his yes.

"To Nana's for Christmas," I said, matching Lily's excitement.

As soon as we stepped inside of Jolie's house, Lily got pulled away by Jolie to put the tree topper on and then help with cookie decorating, and Anthony was stolen by his great-grandparents.

Caleb draped an arm around my shoulders and squeezed me while smiling warmly.

This life had given me challenges and scars, but for

moments like this, I would do it all again. To watch my family smile and laugh together was the greatest joy I could experience.

No matter what life threw at us, I knew we would face it together and that was the best feeling in the world.

Want to read more in this world? Check out Her Royal Harem: Lily.

http://catbanks.co/Lily

CONNECT WITH CATHERINE BANKS

I really appreciate you reading my book! Here are some ways to connect with me:

www.catherinebanks.com

Join my newsletter for deals and snippets:

http://catbanks.co/newsletter

ABOUT THE AUTHOR

Catherine Banks is an award-winning, USA Today bestselling author who writes in several romance subgenres and has multiple pseudonyms. She began writing fiction at only four years old and finished her first full-length novel at the age of fifteen. She is married to her soulmate and best friend, Avery, who she has two amazing children with. After her full-time job, she reads books, plays video games, and watches anime shows and movies with her family to relax. Although she has lived in Northern California her entire life, she dreams of traveling around the world. Catherine is also C.E.O. of Turbo Kitten Industries™, a company with many hats including being a book publisher and store full of nerdy fun.

facebook.com/catherinebanksauthor

BB bookbub.com/authors/catherine-banks

amazon.com/author/catherinebanks

www.ingramcontent.com/pod-product-compliance
Lightning Source LLC
Chambersburg PA
CBHW020440270626
47155CB00022B/699

* 9 7 8 1 9 4 6 3 0 1 7 8 9 *